Dear Sara —
"Venisti, Vidisti, Vicisti!"
♡, Erin Richman

ERIN L. RICHMAN

Josephine
Kathleen
Dottie
Erin
Trish Lee
Elizabeth
Mary Blair (Polly) Cunningham
Mary Blair (Polly) Blakemore
Mary Blair Bryan Peterson
Alexander Marbury Bryan IV
Mary Blair (Polly) Cochran
William
Dorothy Hardy Bryan née Mary Blair Zimmer
Mary Blair (Polly) Zimmer Cochran
Mary Blair (Polly) Pryor Walker Zimmer
Mary Blair (Polly) Pryor Walker
Sara Rice Pryor & Roger A. Pryor

Mary Blair
DESTINY

Copyright © 2019 by Erin L. Richman
All rights reserved.

Printed in the United States of America.
Two Goddesses Publishing.

First printing, 2019

ISBN 978-1-7330180-0-5

www.maryblairdestiny.com

www.facebook.com/themaryblairproject

ERIN L. RICHMAN

This book is based on true events and real people. It reflects the author's present recollections of experiences over time.

Some details have been added, some events have been compressed, and some dialogue has been recreated. The role played by Zimmers in this narrative is entirely fictional. My imagined Polly and Sam do, however, abide by the generally known facts of their lives, and I have sometimes quoted from state records and sworn depositions about these facts. The diary entries… and all the passages relating to Jungian psychoanalysis . . . have no factual basis and are the product of this psychologist's unlicensed imagination.

I would like to thank the real-life surviving members of the family portrayed in this book. I recognize that their memories of the people described in this book may be different than my own. They are each fine, decent, and upstanding people.

If you have read this far, thank you for embarking on this journey into the incredible human lives portrayed in the book, especially that of Dorothy H. Bryan.

Loyalty, strength, and truth
– yours are inspiration for all –

My fierce, beloved Granny,
Dorothy Hardy Bryan,

and

My dear mother,
Anna Bryan Richman.

I hope you find peace in this reclaiming of your story.

ERIN L. RICHMAN

ACKNOWLEDGEMENTS

To my dear Mother, Anna Patricia Bryan Richman, I love you infinitely. I hope my life and work brings honor to yours. You deserve it.

To my inimitable Uncle Marbury, and my strong Aunts Mary Blair, Kathleen, Josephine, Dottie, and Elizabeth: Without your blessing of this project, I would not have even known how to begin it. I cannot begin to express the pride I have in sharing your Mother/Granny's legacy. Thank you for allowing me to tell her story and for your overwhelming love and support.

To my Grandmother, Dorothy Hardy Bryan, for inspiring me every day in your legacy of words and deeds. No amount of gratitude can be fully expressed for your fortitude and remarkable tenacity.

To my Bryan cousins, Pete, Mary Blair, Tommy, Teri, Dorsey, Will, Michael M., Jim P., Michael P., Becky, Renèe, Dan, Mark, Marcy Bryan, Jim B., Allison, Kim, Reina-Marie, Rachel, Bryan, & Chris: We are lucky to share this life on Earth as one tribe. Even as a child, I always bragged about my army of cousins, and still feel so lucky to be 18th of our 24.

To my big sister Sharon for being chairman of the sounding board and chief encouraging officer. To my big sister Karen for always being a proud big sis and sharing your honest opinions.

I would not have started this without urging from Tom Morris, Susan Skidmore, and "Martin" that it was a story worth telling. Thank you all for being such an awesome cheering section and putting up with me.

To Lee Cochran, Lee Dulaney, Neville Blakemore III, I thank you for your warmth and welcoming hearts. Your families created a measure of healing that I could not have imagined was possible. Long live the Lost Tribe of Dorothy!

Thanks for kicking me into gear and encouraging this crazy feat of exploration, my #Profs, Rawlslyn, Beth, and Heidi. I don't know where I would be without you. Thank you for never taking me seriously, and always being so awesome and fabulous.

To Mary Blair Peterson, Amy Baskin and Ashli Archer, your feedback, perspectives, and insights during the writing process were invaluable to me. This work is undoubtedly stronger because of you and the time you took to review and edit my early drafts. Thank you for the largest and tiniest of things you helped to make better. If she were here to do it herself, I am sure Dorothy would thank you, too, for helping me honor her story.

Liz Rice, you created an incredible, amazing, gasp-inducing cover. I do not know how you did it, but I am grateful for your giftedness. Kristin Grandy, thank you for creating the original "split tree" that so beautifully captured the healing from this journey.

To my partner Sara, thank you infinitely for your support and for pushing me to tell this story for my Grandmother. I can never repay you for giving me space to obsess over my obsession and for encouraging me to endeavor into the most fulfilling work I have ever done. Your yin to my yang made this possible.

To my daughters Alex and Cassie, you are loved more than you will ever know. I hope you love with open hearts, and use your brilliant minds to make your time on this Earth special. You breathe in the same air of your foremothers – apply their lessons wisely.

OF MARY BLAIR DESTINY

1

--

Dorothy began life in the arms of strangers. Even they described her as a bright, healthy, energetic, and attractive child. Her parents proudly doted on her.

Dorothy exuded the kind of confidence that one develops from being loved and adored as a child. Throughout her life, she had presence.

She had finished elementary school two years faster than normal. She went off to a private boarding school for Catholic girls and excelled there, too. She came home on weekends to help her mother and to attend Mass at home. Her parents were good, stable people who were known by many in the small town of Indian Head, Maryland, which sat just across the Potomac River from Old Virginia.

Dorothy was an active and industrious young woman, as all who knew her attested. It was fitting, then, that she desired earning power and employment for herself. She would pursue more for herself than other young women her age in the 1920's. Indeed, she was ahead of her time. She turned 18 in June, 1927, and had her sights set on a career in government, pursuing the same livelihood as her parents. Her ambition filled her with desire.

After returning from her senior year of boarding school, she continued her education and earned a business diploma in evening classes at the local public high school back home in Indian Head. In the 1920's, 'business classes' were something young women could do to earn credentials as 'typists.' Dorothy was a skilled pianist and often taught piano lessons to children around town to earn money while she continued to help her mother at home.

It was 1930, the earliest days of what would become the Great Depression, and, for Dot, as she was affectionately called, and everyone else, a government job was a great gig. Civil service jobs with the US government weren't the most exciting work a person could do, but they provided an honest, stable means of income.

In 1930, unemployment was fierce, the U.S. economy had collapsed, and there just weren't enough jobs to go around. Dot was lucky; she actually had a couple of different interviews.

Month after month went by following the interviews, and she heard nothing. She searched for more jobs and interviewed multiple times, still nothing. Finally, after six long months passed, she got an official notice in the mail. After many "thanks, but no thanks" letters that came before, she was both nervous and excited to open this piece of mail, somehow this one felt different.

This special envelope was from The Census Bureau. Inside, she found a letter informing her that she'd been temporarily appointed as a typist at their headquarters. Specific instructions let her know she could report immediately and begin working.

This was Dorothy's big break into the professional world. She got the employment offer before she was even done with her business training, which made her mother proud. This job at the Census Bureau gave her a foot in the door. She leapt at the chance and showed up the next business day, took her civil service oath, and got right to work.

Her determination did not subside after getting this job, Dorothy was never satisfied with "good enough." After only one year she was ready to move up. She got a shot at a promotion to senior typist, but this time for a permanent role, not a temporary one. This promotion meant a real career path, stability, and earning power, all things driving Dot's persistence. She had not one, but two interviews for potential promotions. Either position would be a step up for her, and she was delighted to have two possibilities.

Two obstacles stood in her way: Passing the next level of typist testing and getting selected. Her testing appointment was set for Monday morning, March 23, 1931. This time, she had to go to the D.C. Board of Education a few blocks away from the US Capitol.

So, that sunny but brisk Monday morning on March 23, she trekked to an unfamiliar part of Washington, D.C., not fully sure where she was headed. As she hit the crosswalk at 4th and Indiana Avenue, she spotted the building entrance of the Board of Education. She crossed and melded quickly with the other businessmen and secretaries headed into work on this crisp early spring's morning.

Unknown to her, as she walked toward the building, her feet were stepping on land that shared dust and soil with her birthplace. Of course, she had no idea she'd been born nearby. Indeed, fate brought her back to the exact area – two and a half blocks away – from the precise spot where she was born into this world 21 years earlier. Dorothy took a deep breath, squared her shoulders, and walked right in to the building. She was beaming with confidence.

The world changed the day Dorothy was born, and though she didn't know it yet, it would soon change for her again. She was not only applying for a job, but pushing open a door she had not known was closed.

She took the elevator to the fourth floor, checked in, and began her typing test. With the sound of typewriters clacking, and cigarette smoke wafting through the air of the Education offices, Dorothy quickly finished her test.

"You finished?" the testing proctor asked matter-of-factly and reached out for Dorothy's papers.

"Yes, ma'am, I am," Dorothy smiled.

"Ok, I'll take your papers then. Did you bring your birth certificate?" the lady asked, as if expecting Dorothy to know she was supposed to have it in hand.

"Birth certificate? No, I'm sorry, I didn't bring it," Dorothy said confused.

"Miss Hardy, you see, we need your birth certificate to move you forward for this job. Your parents should have it," the lady said, turning her back to Dorothy signaling she was moving on.

"Ok, thank you, I am sure my parents will have it," Dorothy repeated back as she gathered her purse and coat.

"Get it back to us by the end of the week and you will be okay. Otherwise, we will have to discard your test results," the testing clerk said as she walked away.

Dorothy hurried out of the building and quickly penned a note to her mother, and dropped it at the Post Office.

Dear Mother,
I hope you and Daddy are well. I am writing because I have been asked to furnish a copy of my birth certificate as part of the hiring process at the Board of Education. If you could find it and mail it back to me as soon as you can, that will work. They've told me as long as it gets here this week, they will let me proceed through the hiring process.

Most sincerely yours,
Dorothy

Her mother responded quickly with a short note of her own, but not with the answer Dorothy was wanting.

Dearest Dorothy,
I do apologize, but I do not have your birth certificate here at the house. I will have to write the Maryland Vital Statistics office in Baltimore for it, so I am afraid you won't get it in time for this job. It will take several weeks for me to get it from them. I hope your other interviews go well and I am sorry I don't have better news.

With love,
Mother

That was disappointing. She was completely devastated, but knew she had to act quickly if she was going to find a solution.

This was not going to be simple, after all. Knowing she only had two days left in the week, Dorothy decided to go back to the Board of Education in person to see what her other options were.

Dorothy was determined not to lose this opportunity, so she would go see if there were any other alternatives besides producing a birth certificate. It could not hurt to ask. She went back to the fourth floor, taking the same elevator back up as she did on her previous visit. Perhaps she would find a simple solution.

"Hello, I was here on Monday," Dorothy smiled at the lady clerk who had assisted her two days before. Dorothy was hoping she would remember her quickly.

"I was the one who needed her birth certificate – do you recall my situation, by chance?" Dorothy smiled again, searching for any sign of familiarity in the woman's plain, expressionless face.

"Yes, hello again I recall your visit," the clerk replied, in a flat voice, looking down at the papers she was shuffling.

"You see, I asked my parents for my birth certificate, as you suggested. However, my mother does not have a copy right now," Dorothy spoke clearly and earnestly, hoping to solicit any helpfulness from the clerk.

Dorothy continued, "and she must first write to the Baltimore office. My problem, you see, is that she said it will take several weeks to get it. Do you know if there anything else that will work instead?" Dorothy appealed, hoping for any solution from this counter clerk.

"Oh, I don't know, miss, I just take the forms in and process them. I'll need to ask my supervisor. Can you wait here a minute?" the clerk lady responded curtly.

A couple of minutes later, the clerk returned to the counter, accompanied by a short man wearing a tie, no jacket, and combed-straight, greasy hair. He seemed friendly and earnest, the same pencil-pusher type she'd encountered at other government offices.

He greeted Dorothy with a quick grin, taking over the situation, "Miss, you don't have a birth certificate, I understand. When did you take your typing test?"

"I was here on Monday, Sir," Dorothy replied.

"Monday?" He repeated back to Dorothy.

"Yes, my mother lives in Indian Head, you see, and she told me she can get the birth certificate, but it will take several weeks because she has to request it by mail from Baltimore. I was wondering if there is anything else I can show you instead?" Dorothy asked, trying to be both persuasive and helpful.

"Do you have any relatives here in D.C.?" the supervisor asked.

"Yes, I do, just my aunt and a cousin," Dorothy said, not sure of where he was going with his question.

"What you need is someone to just certify your birth. Just get us a sworn affidavit from your nearest relative in D.C., since your mother can't produce the actual birth certificate in time. Can you do that? Will that work?" he asked.

"Yes, sir, thank you, I can certainly do that. My aunt lives nearby, I am sure she can help me. Thank you very much, sir. I will be back tomorrow," Dorothy said with renewed hope in her voice before turning to walk out. She walked out of the Education Building full of determination to achieve this new mission.

She decided to call Mrs. Annie Darr, her mother's niece, who always gave good practical advice.

Dorothy walked up to a pay phone in the lobby of the building, inserted her nickel, and dialed Annie's number.

"Annie, it's Dorothy. I'm good, thank you. How are you? Good to hear."

Speaking quickly, Dorothy hardly got through the pleasantries before blurting out mid-thought, "I'm in a bit of pickle. You'd think they wouldn't need so much for just applying for a job. It seems they will want a pint of my blood next." Dorothy's tone hinted at her need for assistance, urgency, and feeling of desperation.

"What's wrong, Dorothy, what are you talking about?" Annie quickly replied.

"This job I'm applying for here at the Board of Education. They've asked for my birth certificate; Mother doesn't have it. And I don't have it. They have to have it though," Dorothy explained.

"Oh," Annie said, with quiet concern.

"So, I asked if I can get them anything else instead. They said they'll take a signed statement certifying my birth if it's from a relative. They said I should just ask Aunt Lily," Dorothy continued.

"I can do it for you. I am close enough to your family. I will help you, no problem," Annie quickly offered.

"Are you sure?" Dorothy asked.

"Yes, of course. Just come to my house this evening and we will get it done. OK?"

With that, Dorothy felt the blanket of disappointment lifted.

Later that same evening, instead of going straight to Mrs. Darr's house, Dorothy took a detour. Something in her gut took her to her aunt's house first. Aunt Lily was her mother's sister and was always a supportive, reliable ear for Dorothy. Her Aunt Lily lived in a house in the same neighborhood in Northwest D.C. as Mrs. Darr, so she spontaneously decided to go there first. This quick change of plans would not cost her much time.

Dorothy rode the streetcar to her aunt's neighborhood, and walked the three blocks on the chilly March evening to her aunt's wood, two-story bungalow. When she knocked, Aunt Lily answered and, to Dorothy's surprise, Annie was there, too.

Dorothy looked over at Annie and greeted her with a smile, recognizing she'd interrupted a conversation in progress, as she saw their tea cups nearly emptied.

"Well, hello, my dear! Come on in! Annie is already here; You can join us," Aunt Lily motioned as she welcomed Dorothy in from the cold and took her coat.

"Dorothy, it's good to see your face and not just hear your voice. You've sure been busy lately," Annie exclaimed as she rose to give Dorothy a hug.

Aunt Lily and Annie took their previous seats and immediately brought up the birth certificate issue, as Dorothy settled herself on the couch next to Annie.

"Dorothy, honey, I think it is best that I not attest to your birth since I was not actually present. I'm sorry, dear," Annie's voice trailed off as she patted Dorothy's leg softly and apologetically.

Aunt Lily chimed in, "Dear, only your mother can attest to your birth, but I would be willing to swear that you were born in the United States, if that would work for the Board of Education. I am sure that is all they actually need – to know that you are a natural citizen."

Dorothy was puzzled about the sudden change in plan, and wasn't sure why the issue merited a conversation between them, but brushed the concern out of her mind. Aunt Lily seemed to have a ready-made solution, and that was fine with Dorothy.

"Okay, Aunt Lily, whatever you think is best," Dorothy agreed.

They sat down together and crafted the words.

> *"I hereby attest that Dorothy Stuart Hardy was born in the United States on June 10, 1909, as her mother's sister.*
>
> Signed,
> *Lily Stuart*
> March 25, 1931"

Aunt Lily wrote the affidavit in her own handwriting for Dorothy, and then signed and dated it.

Always the gracious host, Aunt Lily went to work preparing dinner, expecting Dorothy to join her in the kitchen. Annie said her goodbyes and left, leaving Dorothy with alone time working alongside her aunt, finely chopping onions and carrots.

"Aunt Lily, Mother seemed strange the last time I talked with her. She seemed worried about something, preoccupied. She's not normally anxious like that," Dorothy said.

"Oh, what do you mean?" Aunt Lily interjected.

"Something was strange. Is she sick again? Or am I imagining this? Have you noticed anything?" Dorothy asked, referring to her Mother's illness from the previous year.

Dorothy could tell something was worrying her mother – just a gut feeling, nothing specific. She brought it up casually, not expecting her Aunt's speedy affirmation.

"Oh, well, yes, actually. I have noticed. Your Mother is worried about something, but it is nothing for you to be concerned about. You will learn more when it is all settled," Aunt Lily said, without further elaboration.

Dorothy had no idea what "it" was or what needed to be settled, but she trusted her Aunt Lily. In accordance with her dutiful personality, she listened to her aunt's directive and put the apprehension out of her mind. She carried on chopping carrots and let it be.

The next day, she delivered the signed affidavit to the Board, presenting it to the same short, tie-wearing, smiling supervisor whom she'd spoken with the day before. He recognized her as she entered the front office.

"Hello, again, Sir. You might remember we spoke yesterday about my birth certificate. I was able to get my aunt to sign this affidavit, it shows her signature right here," she said, pointing.

"This certifies that I was born in the U.S. Will this work?" She asked, hopefully.

He looked it over, quickly shook his head, and said, "Yes, I believe that should suffice. We'll go ahead and attach it to your other materials and get your application moving forward for further consideration. Looks like we have everything, congratulations, your application is now complete."

"Oh, thank you so much," Dorothy exclaimed excitedly, almost jumping off her feet, while letting out a big exhaled of relief. She turned quickly and walked out of the offices before he could change his mind. As she got back on to the elevator once again, she felt a great sense of relief and hope. She was one step closer to full-time and, more importantly, *permanent* government employment.

ERIN L. RICHMAN

She headed back to her job at the Census Bureau. She was relieved to have this birth certificate headache over and done. All she was looking forward to now was a job promotion.

Dorothy Stuart Hardy, 1927

ERIN L. RICHMAN

2

January, 1909 – Surprise Marriage Delivered D.C. to Petersburg

Sam Zimmer was the son of Petersburg tobacco magnate William L. Zimmer. Their family lived in the old mansion on Sycamore Street as father William thrived at the center of the Petersburg business community. Sam was excited to head off to the University of Virginia for college and Law School in 1904. He had everything figured out. He was going to practice law back in Petersburg, go into politics, and make his father proud following in his big footsteps.

During his stint at UVA, Sam was active and popular, a steady presence in the UVA men's glee club and his fraternity, Delta Kappa Epsilon. He was bright, charming, and had a way with wooing the ladies. The finest young men of Virginia were groomed for adulthood at UVA.

Many were lucky enough to cross paths there with the finest young women of Virginia, too.

Samuel Watts Zimmer was one of those lucky young men when he fortuitously met Polly, a mysterious, strikingly beautiful, intelligent woman. She was four years younger than him, had grown up in Charlottesville and attended UVA, too. She was well-known and alluring, with her raven black hair and deep, dark eyes and olive complexion. She was a captivating young woman with a distinctiveness about her, unmatched by her peers.

Ever since her debut, Polly's life had been a continuous routine of attracting the most eligible men in Virginia and Washington, D.C., and then dismissing them. She always had plenty of admirers in her train, as her beauty was fortified by her wit and a commanding air of aloofness which is so often irresistible to the passion of men. **Though her given birth name was Mary Blair, she was called Polly by all who knew her.**

They met in the summer of 1908, when Polly has just turned 20 and Sam was finishing his law studies.

Polly's Virginia heritage was maybe even more prestigious than Sam's. Her grandmother was a noted author and historian, Sara Rice Pryor, who was publishing books about the likes of George Washington and southerners' lived experiences in the Civil War. Polly's grandfather was a former Confederate General and US Congressman, now the Honorable Roger Pryor, serving as a Supreme Court Justice in New York.

Polly got her middle name, "Pryor," from her grandparents, and her grandmother Sara had a large hand in giving her first name, Mary Blair, as Sara's own grandfather requested in his will that each succeeding generation perpetuate the name of his mother, Mary Blair. Polly's beloved father, Frank Walker, had died a few years before, after surviving the Civil War himself as a Confederate General.

Indeed, Polly was the rare combination of beauty, intellect, and pedigree.

Upon the vast, lush lawns that Thomas Jefferson created, Sam wooed Polly. Jefferson envisioned young minds being enlightened at the University he founded, though surely, many young romances were sparked there as well. Everybody liked Sam, and Polly found herself unable to resist his dashing charm, especially in this idyllic setting, itself designed to induce hope and passion.

Sam was enthralling. He was an ideal admirer – charming, bright-eyed, and popular. He had verve, dash, and exquisite spirit, which made him an enticing beau.

Polly could not have envisioned what would come from their budding romance, yet she allowed herself to dream mightily of a future with Sam. She let her guard down with him that summer, and their passionate courtship extended into the Fall of 1908, near the end of Sam's legal studies at UVA.

Upon learning Polly was carrying his child, Sam would quickly do the right thing by her and marry. After Christmas, they rode separate trains to Washington D.C., and were married on the first Monday following the university's Christmas closures. William Howard Taft had just won the presidency, and Washington was in full swing for its late-winter inauguration of the new President.

On Monday, January 4, 1909, Mary Blair Walker became the wife of Samuel Zimmer, a young Virginia man of great promise. After all, they were married well before the baby was due.

While marriage seemed inevitable, they managed to surprise friends and family by eloping to Washington, forgoing the formal pomp and circumstance that usually accompanied such a high profile union.

They announced their marriage to social circles in Washington and Petersburg. Declared *The Washington Post*:

> "*local society is all agog over the announcement of marriage*" of Polly and Sam.

The *Petersburg Progress-Index* heralded:
> "*the beautiful and accomplished Polly as a welcome addition to the social circles of Petersburg.*"

On January 8, 1909, *Richmond Times-Dispatch* read:

> "*In surprise nuptials, Samuel Watts Zimmer married Mary Blair "Polly" Walker on January 4, in Washington, D.C. The marriage was administered and vows taken at the courthouse in D.C.*"

Though marriage of this promising young couple was celebrated, keen observers certainly knew something was awry. Indeed, their secret baby remained undisclosed in the midst of celebrations for the up-and-coming newlyweds.

Days later, on January 8, their trip back to Petersburg was announced in the Petersburg paper social section:

> "*Mr. S.W. Zimmer and bride arrived late Wednesday night.*"

Three short weeks later, hundreds of family and friends gathered at 244 S. Sycamore Street to attend an extravagant reception in honor of their "recent" marriage. Flowers and servants lined the halls and rooms of the old mansion, inviting curious guests in to celebrate. The party's opulence and elegance masked the hurriedness of the affair. Elaborate décor and prominent guests successfully veiled the urgency for the '*most brilliant social event of the season.*'

In the special "Petersburg News" section in the January 28, 1909, *Richmond Times Dispatch*:

> "The most brilliant social event of the season was the reception given last night at the residence of Mr. William L. Zimmer in honor of his son and daughter-in-law, Mr. and Mrs. Samuel Watts Zimmer, recently married and making Petersburg their home. It was a full-dress, fashionable affair, and one of notable interest. The parlors and rooms of the fine old mansion on South Sycamore Street were handsomely decorated in flowers and the hundreds of guests of the evening represented the culture and refinement, chivalry, and beauty of the city. An elegant and elaborate entertainment was prepared and music was rendered by an orchestra from Richmond. Mr. W.L. Zimmer and Miss Zimmer received, assisted by Mr. and Mrs. Samuel Watts Zimmer, Mrs. James Hay of Washington, Miss Duboise of Charlottesville, and Mrs. Mitchell. Mr. and Mrs. Samuel Watts Zimmer in whose honor the reception was given were very recently married. The bridegroom is a graduate of the University of Virginia, and will practice the profession of law in his native city of Petersburg. The bride, an accomplished and beautiful woman, was Miss Polly Walker, daughter of the late Captain Frank Walker and is the grand-daughter of Judge Roger Pryor of New York [and Mrs. Sara Rice Pryor]. She is a welcome acquisition to the social circles of Petersburg."

Sam stayed in Petersburg and launched his legal career, where opportunities awaited him. Polly, however, could not possibly stay in Petersburg while she was ever-more-pregnant. So, she left for D.C. to stay with her sister Lindsay until she could return to Petersburg without rumor and raised eyebrows from local society. Polly's belly grew, and no one else except Sam and sister Lindsay would know of this pregnancy.

Polly believed Sam when he promised they would have babies and raise them together in marital bliss back home in Virginia. She could not have known then she would bear him four children, and only ever know two of them.

Daylight was short in the midst of winter, and she was still only a few months pregnant, so she disguised her belly and kept any disapprovals at bay for a few months.

By Spring, she and Sam would be in the clear and known as a bona fide married couple. No one would question her being *with child*. The Zimmers were young, beautiful, and in love. Sam was an aspiring lawyer with high hopes for prosperity and power.

As Spring drew to a close, days in Washington grew longer and warmer. The blues and reds in the long evenings' skies gave her plenty to imagine about her future life in Petersburg as her feet traced steps around the Washington Monument. A few new cherry blossoms ringed the tidal basin, as Polly felt the baby's kicks. The tulips' emergence from the Earth reminded her of the delicate life she was growing within her.

By June, Polly was ready as any pregnant mother would be. Her first child was due any day. She could feel the baby moving, anticipating the moment of birth of her first child.

Every movement reminded Polly that new life was imminent and her life was going to change forever. She imagined the wonderful possibilities for her baby. She instinctively longed to settle and nest.

Polly's impending motherhood was evident in her very pregnant belly, yet seriously in question in the mind of Sam, who dreamed about the possibilities of his career.

Sam wanted to seize opportunities in Petersburg. He aspired for greatness and could taste it, even at 24 years of age. Though he was proud to have gotten such a beautiful, well-heeled bride in Polly, he feared the stain of an illegitimate child, conceived out-of-wedlock. This sin and moral failing would tarnish his reputation and threaten legal and political plans.

June arrived. As Polly, the woman who owned the pure, motherly name of Mary Blair, was suffering in the Washington, D.C., summer heat. Sam was also feeling the heat. Little did Polly know she would soon be robbed of the motherhood she spent the past 9 months contemplating.

In the early 1900's, proper young women did not get pregnant before marriage and young couples waited until their wedding night to consummate their love.

Or so society prescribed.

Then, as it is today, young couples took their chances and answered the call of passion more often than anyone dared to admit. Not all of them waited, and not all of them married. The fact was that unmarried men and women were having sex. But the social contract was clear even if it was secretly broken: Good girls waited and only had sex inside the confines of marriage.

Young unmarried women worked to preserve their public images as virgins, and young men were their accomplices. As long as no one got pregnant, there was nothing to worry about.

Self-control was the only birth control. When the only effective contraception was abstinence – well, it surely failed when passions called.

3

Washington, D.C., 1909

Polly was 21, newly married, and pregnant in Washington, D.C. in 1909. Her husband was back home in Petersburg pursuing legal cases and political opportunities.

Polly was not alone, however.

She had her sister, Lindsay, whose residence became home for the next five months until the pregnancy was over. She and Lindsay made for good company which distracted Polly from her reason for being there.

Polly's grandparents, Roger and Sara Pryor, also had a home in Washington for their visits from New York; however, she didn't go to see them that Spring. She could not show herself to them once her pregnant belly began appearing.

She just got 'too busy,' and that excuse seemed to suffice with her grandparents when they came to town. She had left Petersburg after the marriage reception with her well-kept secret. There was no showing yet, and there would be no showing her condition now either.

Lindsay, the *'Mrs. James Hay of Washington'* in the Richmond paper, knew Polly's everything. Lindsay did not approve of the early pregnancy, but she was happy for her sister – and relieved that she'd married.

Lindsay made her home in D.C., but Polly's marriage at D.C. City Hall came as a surprise. Lindsay helped receive the guests at Polly's marriage reception in Petersburg a few weeks later. Lindsay was quite pleased that her new brother-in-law met her high standards. Sam Zimmer, the attorney, would be a great complement to their prominent Virginia heritage, which included the founder of Virginia, Richard Bland, and Thomas Jefferson as distant cousins. Sam was handsome, refined, and well-dressed.

Meanwhile back in Virginia, Polly's parents – Polly and Frank Walker – remained in Virginia despite their daughters' departures for friendlier grounds in the soggy soils of D.C. Their daughters came of age in the boom of the industrial revolution and the economic dominance of tobacco. Money was being made by young men, and prosperity made millionaires of bankers and tobacconists alike. Polly brimmed with hope and promise, but never pictured the path her life was going to take.

Polly carried her name proudly with all of the expectations of fine Virginia aristocratic stock. She was a young woman who would certainly marry at college, bear children for her future husband, and live a long, privileged life in the upper crust of Virginia high society. Perhaps more than any Pryor or Walker daughter, Polly held a shot at redeeming the full wealth and stature her family enjoyed before the South fell.

Polly's future daughter, like her, would be named Mary Blair at her birth and repeat her mother's and grandmother's and great-grandmothers' station in life. Any future son – born of great Virginia pedigree dating back to its very founding as a state – would become a successful Virginia lawyer or businessman and carry forward his parents' sterling legacy.

Polly would have a clear, unfettered path toward her future of predetermined refinement and wealth. This, after all, was the pre-scripted life of a young, fair Virginia woman born of class and privilege.

Having a baby out of timing with her proper marriage, however, was definitely not pre-scripted for Polly's life.

As the 20th century began, Polly was coming of age. She started college at UVA. She cultivated the courtships of the fine fraternity men at UVA. She followed the script.

American society surrounding Polly was in the midst of a vast cultural shift. Preserving southern traditions rested on the shoulders of young women like Polly. Families like hers were intent on saving the ways and traditions of the antebellum Virginia.

In 1909, the U.S. was changing in ways that were new and unfamiliar. Slavery ended decades before, yet Jim Crow was taking hold, especially in the Deep South. Industrial jobs began to replace farm work and ushered in millions of immigrants to work in factories. Yet, tobacco manufacturing shielded many Virginians from economic downturns.

Polly was protected from all of this. She may have come of age in the 20th century, but her world was steeped in tradition, heritage, and formality. Country clubs, social life, debutante balls, and society weddings defined her world – and all were underpinned by a strict code of chastity before marriage. In the worlds of the most wealthy and privileged, the Victorian era was still very much alive, guiding and preserving Americans' definitions of all that was *good* and *right*.

In the peak of Polly's youth, women wore dresses, covering their corsets, slips, and brassieres. Bodies were concealed. Skin was covered so as not to tempt the attention of men. When their fair skin was revealed, it was intentional and alluring.

The term *fine woman* was used to describe a woman's chastity and virginal quality. Fine-ness implied purity and all that was virtuous and good.

Indeed, a fine woman – a *good* woman – was surely a virgin when she married, and there existed an unspoken social understanding that her husband would save his sexual cravings for a mistress; the wife was much too pure to do anything but have sex for the purpose of making a baby.

Carnal, dirty, lusty, and pleasure sex might corrupt her purity, a purity that must be preserved and protected so that she could be the most loyal wife and most wholesome of mothers. And as a good Southern woman, she would maintain her cheerfulness, of course.

Women could not vote, and women of status did not work. They had servants, or *domestics* who were responsible for household labor. Teen girls had coming out balls, and social clubs for debutantes. Social visits were announced in the newspaper. This was the world in which Polly came of age, and one that would define her and her sisters' lives.

--
Newlywed Polly Makes the Most of D.C.

Born in 1888, after the Civil War, young Polly was part of a generation expected to preserve the traditions of Old Virginia and status of wealthy White Southerners displaced by the South's loss of the War. Sara, her grandmother, was a perfect exemplar of these values.

Grandmother Sara wrote volumes venerating Virginia life and culture before its fall following the Civil War. Her granddaughters' generation of young mothers were expected to use these treatises as teachings to restore Virginia's stature to the plantation era. Southern granddaughters would comply by exhibiting distinctively Southern feminine grace and cheer, but also by raising their children to view the War of Northern aggression as the monumentally unjust assault on Southern states' rights.

Through her grandparents, Polly was no stranger to stories of fleeing. Virginia was no safe place for a former Confederate General and his wife to remain after emancipation. Though her grandparents fled to New York after the war, most of their adult children remained in Virginia and adapted to the new South.

Polly and Lindsay expected to remain and preserve their grandparents' status atop society. They grew up with multiple servants, as was common for southern white people of the upper class. Their grandparents even took their servants to New York with them when they fled Virginia. Loss of place did not mean loss of status to the likes of Pryors.

Lindsay's husband was as adventurous as Polly was ambitious. Lindsay's husband, James Hay, Jr., was an aspiring writer. They had been married in Charlottesville a few years before relocating to Washington, D.C.

James and Lindsay settled. into their apartment building in northwest D.C. on 918 18th Street NW, just a few quick blocks down from the White House and Washington Monument. They were in the thick of all things D.C.

James' father was a congressman from Virginia, just as Lindsay's grandfather Roger Pryor had been. An innate understanding of Washington-Virginian politics was in their blood. They'd observed their parents and grandparents win elections, and they knew how to float amongst the flux of the Washington elite.

James and Lindsay were a 'son' and 'daughter' couple of the revolution – literally and figuratively. They could enjoy the spoils of their parents' status in stable and prosperous industrial America. Indeed, they were rare beneficiaries of two generations of roll-up-your-sleeves-politicking in what was a new and untested democracy.

Lindsay and James' apartment location was perfect for him, as it put him within walking distance to the White House. His job with the *Washington Times* granted him frequent access to candidate-turned-President William Taft, who James covered in political columns.

In fact, James spent most of 1908, 1909, and 1910 travelling with President Taft, who rescued him from newspaper work. Taft gave James prime interviews and up-close access to his administration. Later, James formed an enduring friendship with President Woodrow Wilson.

President Taft's inauguration in January 1909 was the wintriest ever seen. Temperatures were frigid and the D.C. air was filled with powder white snow. James wasn't home much then, or really ever.

It was an exciting time in the Hay household, as the couple was swept into the ritual of the Presidential inauguration in D.C.

Polly's extended stay in their apartment was hardly noticed. Sam's quick return to Petersburg was hardly noticed either. Sam and Polly's swift marriage was hardly competition for Presidential politics and inaugural events. Polly kept Lindsay company when James was absent. All was well.

Most young reporters only dream of having such unfettered access to a President, and James had it. His friends, Woodrow Wilson and William Taft, kept him bouncing between New York and D.C. James quickly moved on from writing for Washington newspapers and magazines and began shopping his books and plays in New York City. His work life was an adventure and kept him traveling constantly.

Sam and Polly's agreed-upon plans were - *go straight to Washington and get married, and then figure out how and where to raise the baby*. By his math, Sam figured the baby was due in early Summer, so they still had several months to truly decide on a plan. Polly was fine with going to D.C., if it pleased Sam, thinking that her dream of having his baby and becoming a mother would soon become her reality.

Lindsay's husband, James Hay, meanwhile, was starting a new social club to advance his journalism career, the fledgling *National Press Club*. When he was home, however, he was one of the only witnesses to Sam and Polly's pregnancy drama. With a reporter's eye for detail and a capacious memory, he was aghast at the Walker-Zimmer families' obsession with concealing the truth, no matter the cost.

ERIN L. RICHMAN

OF MARY BLAIR DESTINY

4

Mother Battlefield: The Polly Pedigree

Polly embodied the promise of her proud family and their potential return to prominence. Her family was rebuilding like the rest of Virginia after their homes, assets, and status were lost amid the ashes of the Civil War. Polly's grandparents, Roger and Sara Pryor, lost everything after the war, including their Petersburg home. He was a General present for the first shots at Fort Sumter and the surrender of Richmond at the war's end. Unsurprisingly, the post-War South was no longer a hospitable place to former Confederate Generals and those mourning antebellum Virginia.

Pryor lineage remained special in Virginia nonetheless. The Pryor family surname came with such high regard that young Pryor women retained it, as several Pryor daughters also did with the Walker family surname after marrying. For example, when Lindsay and Polly's mother, Mary Blair Pryor married, she merely became Mary Blair *Pryor* Walker. Likewise, when the daughters married, they simply became Lindsay *Pryor Walker* Hay and Mary Blair "Polly" *Pryor Walker* Zimmer.

Sara Pryor's Order of Mary Blairs

The name Polly also had a distinctive history which was originated by Sara Pryor. Sara began this tradition when she named one of her daughters Mary Blair in honor of her own aunt, Mary Blair. Though called "Mary Blair" as their formal, legal name, "Polly" was the informal nickname for their friends and family. The unique name, Mary Blair, and its nickname "Polly" became an honorific for Sara's progeny. Two of Sara's granddaughters would also be named Mary Blair, sprouting branches of Mary Blairs.

These Mary Blairs – Sara Pryor's Mary Blairs – carried the tradition forward and would name their daughters Mary Blair "Polly" for several decades. The Mary Blair name would be carried forward into perpetuity – as a testament to Sara's adoration for her aunt and adoptive mother.

MRS. ROGER A. PRYOR.

The name Mary arouses thoughts of *purity* and, of course, the holy mother. Blair sounds refined and sophisticated. Matched with Mary, however, Blair sounds even more ethereal than it does alone.

What is this name, Mary Blair? Broken down by its literal definition, Mary Blair means 'mother battlefield'. Mary = mother of Jesus. Blair = battlefield.

Mother battlefield. It is doubtful that Sara Rice Pryor thought of this meaning when naming her daughter "Mary Blair."

Why was the name so important to Sara?

As a strong, resilient mother in her own right, Sara ensured that her daughters would carry the matrilineal name forward in their daughters.

Sara herself was the youngest of 12 children. Her mother was fertile, but too ill and frail to raise her. So, in 1833, at age three, she was sent to live with her Aunt Mary Blair and Uncle Sam Hargrave in Hanover, Virginia.

Going to live with Aunt Mary Blair and Uncle Sam meant travelling by horse-drawn carriage through the hills of Virginia. Sara's aunt and uncle soon loved their special niece as their own daughter, as they had never had any children. Aunt Mary Blair and Uncle Sam made sure she had all of the best opportunities in her young life.

In her own right, Aunt Mary Blair was a woman of strong mind, independence of thought, and devoted piety, as well as a tolerance far ahead of her time. She reared young Sara with all of the advantages that would be given to an only daughter. Aunt Mary Blair gave Sara a love of life, an innate curiosity, and a love for words, literature, music, and history. She took great joy in leading Sara into the world of culture, and, in later years, she also did the same for Sara's children.

Mary Blair took special care of Sara, and, to Sara's good fortune, even relocated so that she could receive a better education in Charlottesville, where the University of Virginia set high standards for its community. She exposed Sara to French literature, dance, and expert lessons on the piano in Bach, Chopin, Von Weber, and Beethoven. Sara's childhood with Aunt Mary Blair was a time of "absolute serenity and happiness," she wrote in her memoir.

Sprung from this enriched childhood, Sara developed a deep love and admiration for her Aunt Mary Blair. They had a profound bond. Aunt Mary Blair became her mother by adoption, and Sara treasured her throughout her life. When Sara's marriage took her away from the home of her childhood, she began to lay the foundation of her future authorship in letters to Aunt Mary Blair. Wishing to surmount the separation between her and her adopted mother, she took Aunt Mary Blair into every detail of her life while they were away from each other via her written word.

As they saw no future in their burned out, war-ravaged Virginia, the Pryors moved north in 1868 with nothing but the clothes they were wearing. They started over from scratch in New York City, working in whatever way they could to earn money and support themselves and their youngest children. To their surprise, they found New York City to be a welcoming place for charming southerners such as them, giving Sara and Roger the chance to re-establish themselves after the trauma of the Civil War.

While Roger practiced law, Sara began writing, doing charity work, and supporting Roger's restarted career. It took years of toil and worry, stripped of the advantages they enjoyed in pre-War Virginia, but the Pryors regained their once-lost prominence. Eventually, the Pryors amassed enough money, and moved from Brooklyn to uptown Manhattan. They established themselves among the New York elite as Roger's law practice grew. His legal achievements eventually earned him a place on the New York State Supreme Court.

He would become known as Justice Pryor for the remainder of his years. She would become known as philanthropic leader in New York, even raising money for a yellow fever outbreak in Jacksonville, Florida. The public's memory of their time in the confederacy would fade. Together, the couple healed their painful scars from war and sincerely fully embraced the saving of the Union and fall of the Confederacy.

At age 73, Sara wrote her first of several novels and memoirs. She dedicated her final novel, *The Colonel's Story (1911)*, to her beloved adoptive mother Mary Blair:

To the Memory

OF

MY DEAR ADOPTIVE MOTHER

MARY BLAIR HARGRAVE

TO WHOM I OWE ALL THAT I AM

AND MAY HOPE TO BE

Sara's contributions to the public discourse about the Civil War and her work on the American Revolution led to her emergence late in life as an influential source for historians. Privately, her love for her Aunt Mary Blair influenced generations of women, and prompted the source of their names.

First among Sara Pryor's branch of Mary Blair's was her daughter, Mary Blair Pryor, who, naturally, also carried the nickname Polly. After marrying General Frank Walker, Polly became Mary Blair "Polly" Pryor Walker (I). She kept her maiden name in her legal name because the Pryors were so esteemed throughout Virginia, Washington, and New York. Retaining the Pryor name preserved great social value.

Polly Pryor Walker gave birth to her daughter to Mary Blair Pryor Walker, and called her Polly (II). Polly (II) then got married to a fine young Virginian man named Sam Zimmer, and, thus, became Mary Blair "Polly" Pryor Walker Zimmer. Her name was quite as close to regal as an American can get.

And Polly kept every part of her mother's name. *Mary Blair "Polly" Pryor Walker Zimmer*.

And there was also Mary Blair Rice, granddaughter to Sara Pryor and a niece to Polly Pryor Walker. She became a best-selling author, and also world-famous geographer, quite a rarity for a woman of her day.

Mary Blair Rice, aka *Blair Niles*

Mary Blair Rice made her home in New York City when she was not traveling the globe to Africa, the Caribbean, and South America. She was also the first woman to spend time on Devil's Island, a Caribbean penitentiary. She spent months living amongst and interviewing its prisoners for her research. Using this incredible experience as its basis, she wrote a novel and screenplay, *Condemned to Devil's Island*. Her legal name remained Mary Blair, though she published under her pen name, "Blair Niles," based on the last name of her second husband, Robert Niles, Jr.

Sara Pryor, the writer and grandmother, surely must have been proud of her writer-granddaughter, who not only wrote, but traveled the globe commissioning all of the enrichments of culture, art, and literature that Sara once shared with her Aunt Mary Blair and children alike.

Naming a female baby for her mother was as uncommon and unique then as it remains today. Even more remarkable is its continuity across multiple generations. The name – *Mary Blair* – is extraordinarily unique and regal. In all, there were three Mary Blairs alive in 1900, all created from Sara Pryor.

More than any, perhaps Polly Walker held her grandmother's hopes for elite redemption back home in Virginia. In early Fall, 1908, Polly was a University of Virginia student, studying in the same town where her famous grandmother had been reared. By no accident, Polly walked on the same hallowed Jeffersonian grounds as her grandmother Sara when Sara was still young. Charlottesville was carefully chosen by old school Virginians for its exquisite enrichments. Sam was also finishing his legal studies at the University of Virginia after having earned his Bachelor's degree there as well. His then-girlfriend Polly was captivating, and her pedigree preceded her.

Polly must have realized she was pregnant sometime between the changing of leaves' color in late fall and Christmas. She surely told Sam as soon as she knew.

They knew they could get through family Christmas events without anyone noticing or knowing. Certainly, grandmother Sara would not know of this. No other Mary Blairs would know of this, either.

OF MARY BLAIR DESTINY

5

--
A Secret's Destiny in D.C. – June 1909

For the last time, Sam left Petersburg on the evening train headed to Washington. His visits to D.C. would be coming to an end soon, and he still hadn't figured out how to bring Polly back to Petersburg with a baby.

His last case had just wrapped up in court, and his new work life was going incredibly well.

"This is just the first step for you, Sam." Sam's father told him. William expected his son to excel and share the reins of the family dynasty with his other son, Billy.

William Sr.'s expectations for his son needn't be explained; his sons' lives were tracked for status and power since they were in diapers. The Zimmer family sat atop Petersburg society with few others. Sam and Billy were the heirs-apparent of their father's power-base.

Yet the only thing on Sam's mind as he boarded the train was what to do about this baby. It was finally time. He knew this. But he surely didn't know how he would tell his father, William, Sr., that he was married already AND had a baby. He could not. He simply could NOT.

Bringing a baby home from D.C. was inconceivable.

The prospect of bringing a baby back to Petersburg contradicted the future they were planning to build. He was hit like a bolt of lightning every time the baby entered his mind. His fists and jaw clenched. The bright young lawyer had no solution for his most daunting problem.

Sam did not tell anyone, not even his brother Billy, about the pregnancy. No one knew the real reason why his new wife, Polly, was truly staying in D.C. with her sister Lindsay. Billy was both his brother and his friend, but the risk of William Sr. finding out was too great.

Sam surely could not disappoint his father, and it was utterly unimaginable how his new wife *plus surprise baby* would come with him to live in Petersburg. The situation was impossible.

The hiding of the true reason for their marriage had now grown into an unavoidable lie. As a man of status and privilege, it came naturally to Sam to make decisions – whether to solve problems or dispose of problems. He was accustomed to making decisions with authority.

In the final hours of Polly's pregnancy, Sam's four-hour train ride alone gave him enough time to play out various scenarios. One option: He, Polly, and baby could just move somewhere. They could re-establish themselves and raise the baby far away from the judgment of the Petersburg elite.

He discarded this option quickly. This would mean he would detach from his entire family – his father, his mother, his sisters and his brother. Most importantly, escaping judgment in a new town would mean leaving behind the family dynasty and his emerging political opportunities.

As another option, he could surrender the baby to an orphanage for adoption. He quickly discarded this idea, too. He knew Polly would never agree to give the baby away, and it was not worth stepping on this landmine with his new wife. Perhaps above all else, he absolutely wanted no record attaching his name to this baby. Formally giving the baby up was not an option.

His thoughts raced. He made lists of pros and cons. The train barreled northward to Union Station.

Finally, he convinced himself of the solution before his train crossed the Potomac River that evening. As he stepped down the metal steps of the train onto the platform, he knew exactly how he would fix this.

Sam walked up to 223 C Street. He held Polly's elbow as they approached a two-story boarding house in a part of D.C. that in no way resembled the mansions they were accustomed to in Virginia.

It was dark out, and Sam thumped on the door authoritatively despite the late hour. A light flicked on from inside the doorway, and the landlady answered, a short, stocky older woman. The heavy door creaked open just a few inches – enough for the landlady to get a look at the disruptors to her evening.

"Excuse me, ma'am, sorry to bother, but would you have a vacancy for me and my pregnant wife?"

"How many nights do you need?" the landlady replied, looking Sam over and recognizing he was well-dressed, clean-shaven and well-bred.

"Just one. Maybe two. But that's all."

"Do you know how late it is?" the older woman admonished him.

"Yes, ma'am, I am sorry, I do. My wife here is pregnant and we need a place for her to rest for the night, as we are from out of town," Sam said, smiling, earnestly trying to charm her into letting them inside. Tapping into a woman's sympathies for another woman is always a sure bet, as Sam well knew.

"It will be $7 for tonight, payable in cash in advance," she peppered.

"Not a problem, ma'am. I have cash right here. May we come in and rest now?" Sam pleaded.

"She looks very pregnant. Is she okay?" the woman asked, noticing Polly breathing hard, wincing and turning away in pain.

"Yes, she is fine. I think she might have just not eaten well at supper," Sam said as he pulled Polly toward him and took a step over the threshold.

Sam knew Polly was not fine. The secret baby was coming. Sam needed to secure a room so his plan could move forward.

He'd decided on his train ride up that this baby would remain a secret. There was no other option. He would take Polly into the shadows of a skid-row boarding house, give the baby away as soon as it was born, and return to his budding political career in Petersburg.

"Here's your room. Bathroom's at the end of the hall, 10-minute limit there. Any questions?" the lady mumbled, as if saying it for the 99th time, and motioned Sam and Polly into their private room on the second floor.

"Thank you, that's all we need," Sam replied.

As the door shut, he took Polly's shawl and walked her to the bed.

"Go ahead and lie down, get some rest," Sam said to Polly.

"Sam, they're getting stronger," Polly moaned, referring to her contractions.

She was now in the 9th hour of labor. She knew there wasn't much time left. She was sweating profusely in the June heat, breathing so hard she nearly fainted.

"Sam, we need a doctor, and now!" she implored.

Sam ran downstairs, interrupting the lady's evening again. He thumped on her private door. She unlatched the locks, and opened the door, seeing it was the charming-yet-late gentleman again.

"What is it?" She groaned.

"Ma'am, I am sorry to bother again, but it seems my wife is in labor. Would you happen to have the telephone number of a doctor who could come to check her?" Sam pleaded again.

In disbelief, and seeing she'd been duped, she answered, "Are you kidding me?"

"No, ma'am, I am telling you the truth. I need the number of a doctor, and I'd like to use your telephone, please." Sam voice was firm and directing.

She knew he was serious. She saw it in Polly's eyes on the front doorstep. She wasn't one to judge, yet she was irritated by Sam's deceit.

"Hold on a minute," she said, and shut her door.

Two minutes went by. Sam waited in the foyer, wondering if she would have a doctor for him. Either way, he was committed to his plan. There would be no official birth, whether he himself delivered the baby or a doctor did.

Suddenly, the door opened, and she stretched out a piece of paper with a name and number scribbled on it.

"Dr. Lawrence. He can help. Telephone is at the end of the hall on the left. Keep it quiet so you don't disturb everyone else in this house," she admonished.

Sam walked to the end of the hall, and called the number on the paper. No answer. He called two more times. Finally, on the third dial, a groggy voice answered.

"Hello," the deep voice of a man answered.

"Is this Dr. Lawrence?" Sam asked the phone.

"Yes, it is, who is this?" the groggy voice answered.

"Kind sir, I am Sam Brant, and I am in town tonight with my wife, who is very pregnant, and appears to be in a lot of pain with labor. Is there any way possible you could come to 211 C Street for a house call?" Sam pleaded.

Without skipping a beat, Sam made up a fake last name for the doctor.

"She's pregnant? How many months?" the doctor asked.

"I am not sure, Dr. Lawrence. But she is very pregnant and I am fairly certain she is in labor. Can you come now? 211 C Street Northwest." Sam begged.

The doctor sighed and agreed, "Yes, I am gathering my things and will head your way. It will take me a bit to summon a carriage at this hour."

"Please hurry, and thank you," Sam urged him, with relief.

Dr. Lawrence was no stranger to the neighborhoods of Washington. He'd been making house calls all over the district for over a decade when he began his general practice following graduation from George Washington University's medical school. He lived not far from C Street, where he also ran his boarding house, renting to another physician, a lawyer and a couple of federal government professionals.

His new nurse, Nellie, also rented a room from him in his large Northwest D.C. boarding house. She had already prepared his bag that evening for any potential house calls. His journal and supplies were ready to go. He grabbed his bag, his hat, and headed out his front door. In the June's evening darkness, he walked across the soil and brick just a hundred feet over to the still-busy Massachusetts Avenue.

The carriage briskly moved down Massachusetts through the humid summer air. He quickly arrived to the address Mr. Sam "Brant" had provided on the telephone. Dr. Lawrence walked up to the front door of the C street boarding house, one much less clean than his own, he noted. As any doctor appearing for a house call, he was not sure what awaited him inside.

Sam greeted the doctor with a "hello" from the end of the hallway, just as the front door was opening 16 feet away.

"Hello, Dr. Lawrence, thank you for coming. I'm Sam," Sam quickly met the doctor's eyes with his own while motioning toward the doorway of his rented room.

Dr. Lawrence had never had seen a man so mentally distressed over a situation like this. Sure, he had seen other young couples 'in trouble' over the years, but none like this. Sam's demeanor was different.

"Hello, ma'am, I am just going to check you and make sure all is well. We will take care of you," Dr. Lawrence assured Polly, and introduced her to Nellie, his nurse.

After checking Polly, who was clearly in advanced labor, the doctor set down his bag and stood up. This was a routine delivery and the baby was due shortly, he explained.

"Are you married?" the doctor asked, making eye contact with Polly.

"We are married, yes," Sam interjected from behind when the doctor asked if he was the young woman's husband. Polly didn't speak, and it was clear Sam was in control.

"You're going to be okay," Dr. Lawrence's nurse, Nellie, whispered as she wiped Polly's forehead with a cool, wet cloth to comfort her, distracting her from Sam and the doctor. Polly was nervous yet ready, like any expectant young mother awaiting delivery of her first baby.

The room was small, humid and hot in the Washington D.C. summer swelter. Sam walked to the doorway to get some air, and turned back to face the doctor.

"Sir, might I have a word with you in the hall while the nurse stays with my wife?" Sam motioned to Dr. Lawrence with a polite flick of his head.

"Everyone is a little nervous with the first, young man. You said you're married, right?" Dr. Lawrence said as he offered Sam a cigarette.

"Oh, yes, of course, doctor. We were married in January right here in Washington."

"Well, what do you do for a living, Mr. Brant?"

"I am a lawyer practicing down in Petersburg. Just finished at UVA last year, sir. I have big plans," Sam answered, with his tone suggesting this evening was not part of those plans.

Sam took a long pull on the freshly lit cigarette.

"We can't take the baby with us, doctor," Sam exhaled.

The doctor stopped and looked up at Sam, confused.

Sam added, strangely, "But we are planning to move west and settle soon. And we can come back in a few weeks to get the baby, for sure."

Silence.

The doctor stared at Sam, stunned at what he'd just heard.

He'd seen other babies born into 'troubled' situations, but none where the parents simply left a healthy baby.

Dr. Lawrence thought to himself, "What kind of decent human is able to abandon a newborn baby?"

"Take care of it until we move, we have to get ready to move out west." Sam said to the Doctor. Sam knew that was a lie. He had no intention of moving out west. But the little lie about moving made the bigger lie possible: He had no intention of ever reclaiming the baby.

The doctor looked at him stupefied. "You want me to do what?"

Who says "Take care of the baby until we move?"

It didn't add up.

"You what?" Dr. Lawrence said again, quizzically.

He wants to leave his newborn with a stranger? To hand it over, freely, without wondering who will care for it and how its needs will be met?

"I can't take the baby with us," Sam spoke clearly without hesitating. As the words left his lips, he knew this was what must happen.

"Don't you – isn't there someone you know who can take care of the baby? A servant? I can pay for its care." Sam continued.

"You don't just leave your baby, sir. That's not how this works," Dr. Lawrence admonished.

"Doctor, you must understand, I will come back for the baby in a few weeks when we make our out way out west. I simply cannot take it now with me back to Petersburg. I simply cannot. You must understand this," Sam implored.

"You said you aren't worried about legitimacy. What's the problem? I thought you said you two are married," Dr. Lawrence pressed.

"We were married in January, yes. Of course, the baby is legitimate," he scoffed. "But it is coming a bit too early. We cannot bring the baby home to Petersburg and have questions. You understand?" Sam said, matter-of-factly.

Of course, Sam knew what awaited them in Petersburg. And Sam knew he would never return for the baby. He just needed to get out of D.C. without it – that was the task at hand.

"She's still got a bit to go before the baby arrives. Just take a walk and you will calm yourself down," the doctor tried encouraging Sam.

Hours passed. No baby. Polly's contractions continued, as did her pain and moans. Sam paced the floor, smoking cigarettes to keep his nervous hands occupied.

Lunch time came and went, but no one ate. Polly was crying in pain during what seemed to be the last moments of labor. The doctor administered medication to relax her, which put her into a sleep-like state, just as the baby's head was crowning.

Her pain ceased. She seemed half-asleep. Her body did the rest of the work of labor without her being conscious for the birth.

Sam stood in the hall while the baby's head, shoulders, and body made its exit from Polly's body. He knew she had taken her first breaths when he heard the baby's cries from the hallway.

Polly remained dazed, unaware of the baby's presence.

The doctor cleaned the baby. He cut the cord. He proceeded with checking it for pulse, temperature, and alertness. He observed it to be a healthy baby girl, ten fingers and toes, and breathing well.

The nurse cooled Polly's forehead with a damp cloth as she rested. Sam listened from the hall.

A few minutes later, the doctor emerged from the room, holding the newborn in his arms.

"Here's your daughter, Sam," the doctor said, showing the baby girl to the new father.

Sam stood there, looking, but kept his hands in his pockets. He did not reach out to hold the baby. He did not smile at the infant. He maintained eye contact with the doctor.

"I need you to keep her until we settle, Doctor," Sam repeated what he'd said before, without looking twice at the baby.

"Don't you want her to see the baby first? Maybe just take a breath and calm down a bit. You are just nervous. Every man is," the doctor said, trying to divert Sam's attention and ease his urgency.

"No, I do not. She is not to see the baby," Sam said, matter-of-factly, growing frustrated with the doctor's insistence.

Dr. Lawrence had seen a lot in his years, but this was a new one, even for him.

"I am adamant, sir. Do not take that baby back in there," Sam demanded, stepping in front of the doorway when he saw the doctor's eyes glance toward the room at where the new mother lay resting, half-unconscious.

"What do you propose I do with it? It is not my baby, it is yours," the doctor probed.

"Just take it until we settle. I will pay for its care until we can come back, which we will do on our way out west," Sam's repetition was convincing, using his lawyering skills.

Sam eventually convinced the doctor to take the baby away before Polly awoke and promised to send $10 a month by money order to cover its care and support.

Dr. Lawrence left the house, letting Sam and Polly leave D.C. without the newborn infant. Sam's plan was complete, and the baby was out of his hands. Instead, Dr. Lawrence had an unsolicited problem in his hands.

Arriving home from the house call, Dr. Lawrence appeared in the doorway with a newborn swaddled in a blanket. This was not what Dr. Lawrence's wife, Bessie, expected. They were already raising a 6-year-old daughter, and had no plans for another.

"Albert, what in the world?" Bessie inquired of the newborn in her husband's arms.

"I know. It was the most bizarre house call I've ever made, Bessie. I've never encountered a man in such distress. It was incredibly strange. He wouldn't let the mother see her baby. He said they couldn't take it home with them, and yet he said they'd come back in a few weeks to get her. They were from Virginia. The woman was so pretty. I just don't understand what was happening," he stammered, tired and dizzy from the past few hours.

"How did YOU end up with their baby?" she asked with confusion. He had never come home with a baby after a house call. He had never come home looking so distressed like this.

He explained what had transpired at the C Street boarding house from the moment he arrived to the moment he left with a baby. He explained that Sam said he would come back in several weeks when on their way to moving out west.

"Something seemed very off, Bessie, and I felt like he gave me no choice," Dr. Lawrence was stupefied.

They discussed at length what to do next. They recounted tales of children lost to orphanages and kidnappers. Orphanages in D.C. were crowded with parentless children, staffed by unregulated keepers and governesses. One Catholic orphanage, St. Ann's, took infants, but together they decided that an orphanage was absolutely out of the question. What happened to a baby once it entered an orphanage was too chilling to imagine.

Dr. Lawrence and his wife were both fully aware of yet another sordid alternative – one that they agreed they absolutely wanted to protect baby Mary Blair from no matter what. An underground black market of baby selling was alive and well in D.C. and Maryland. Babies were taken surreptitiously from hospitals, and then sold to an underground trafficking network that dealt in babies. Infants and children were kidnapped, sold many times into indentured servitude, and disappeared forever. Sometimes they were transported via trains to farms in the Midwest, only to grow up in servitude working the farms.

The Lawrence's wanted to avoid this underbelly of city life for vulnerable children. Protecting the abandoned infant from all of the very real dangers of kidnapping and baby trafficking meant they had to handle the matter themselves. Mr. Sam "Brant" promised he would come back, and, though they did not ask for this duty, they protected the baby so her prominent parents could reclaim her when they returned.

When the baby was two weeks old, Dr. Lawrence and his wife arranged for the baby girl to be cared for by Sarah Watson. They were very familiar with Mrs. Watson and trusted her completely. Though she was 66 years old, she still occasionally cared for and boarded sick babies who were in Dr. Lawrence's care.

They explained to Mrs. Watson that the baby's parents were a prominent Virginia couple who would be back soon to retrieve the baby. Her care would be only for a short term. With Mrs. Watson, the baby would be safe and cared for, and they could rest their minds about the responsibility they felt.

Mrs. Watson was reliable and independent, living behind a small confectionery that she ran in Southeast D.C. She lived with her daughter, Ida Cleary, Ida's husband, and their son, Howard. They all shared living costs in the two-story apartment where Mrs. Watson stayed on the first floor in the back of her confectionery.

She agreed to keep the baby on the condition that the financial support came through regularly, as she could not afford to care for a baby using her own scarce resources. Mrs. Watson did not care about making profit, she just needed funds to meet the baby's basic needs for food and clothing. She would not charge for giving the baby love, just for her basic necessities.

As the weeks and months went by, Mrs. Watson became attached to the baby girl, showering her with affection. She kept a single picture of her framed on her dresser. She did not have much, but she was kind and generous with what she had.

With Mrs. Watson taking on the role of mother, the baby was out of the doctor's hands. And Sam's problem was solved, too – for now.

Dr. Lawrence spent many evenings that June walking and pacing every evening. The sidewalks he gazed down upon had no answers for the anxiety he had. His doctor and lawyer friends warned him about being involved in this situation at all, yet he continued to guard the baby. He treated her colds, fevers, and ear aches, monitoring her health and welfare as she passed new milestones and popped her first teeth.

For Dr. Lawrence, June's sunsets were vivid in 1909. His house calls would never be the same. He would never be the same.

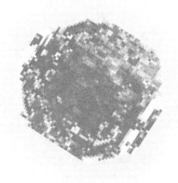

6

Dreams on South Sycamore Street

Polly's memory of giving birth in the rented boarding room was quickly being obscured by her new life as Mr. Sam Zimmer's wife. After the baby was born, Sam whisked Polly back to Petersburg on the train. The baby was hurriedly left behind to be cared for at first by the delivery doctor and whomever else the doctor knew who was willing to foster the abandoned baby.

Meanwhile, Sam and Polly settled into their home next door to his mother and father, a home beautifully decorated for the young couple's arrival that summer. Polly began her new life as a Zimmer, and assumed her role in Petersburg society. Her sisters-in-law lived nearby as well, and they happily introduced her to the young women in Petersburg's graceful social circles. She inherited a new domestic servant to help her with whatever she needed at home.

No doubt, in those first few weeks, Polly was wading in and out of mansion parlors. She was navigating the women's lounges as the 'new girl' at Petersburg Country Club. Yet, she was also recovering from giving birth, a fact she could conceal from everyone but herself.

Indeed, no woman's body lets her birth a baby without reminding her that she is no longer pregnant. Polly was most certainly experiencing sharp post-birth uterine contractions and bleeding in the days immediately following the secret baby's delivery. She had every post-pregnancy readjustment. Milk was entering and engorging her breasts, as it naturally would, but with no baby to extract it for her. All of the normal post-partum hormonal rebalancing – instead of being a soft landing, was more like a plane crash.

Her body was returning to its pre-pregnancy state, but she had no baby to dote on or project her maternal instincts. Her body – and her mind – quietly shut the door on a pregnancy that no one else would know about. She talked to no one about this loss. Lindsay was back in D.C., not by her side every day to distract her from her woes.

No one would glean from her attractive demeanor that she had just given birth. For Polly, an "attractive demeanor" meant looking beautiful, plus entertaining lively conversations, possessing good cheer, and honoring her exceptional Virginia lineage. Despite her physical reminders of recent birth, she impressed her new friends and carried on with her social duties as Sam's wife.

Sam announced his candidacy for elected office just days after they returned from D.C. On June 24, the newspaper announced Sam was the only candidate from Petersburg for the Virginia House of Delegates.

"We fully endorse Sam Zimmer as our sole nominee from Petersburg," local party leaders announced.

As anticipated, Sam won that seat and served in the Virginia legislature for several years.

A few days later at the start of July, Sam's $10 payment arrived in the form of a Western Union Money Order, addressed "c/o Dr. Albert

Lawrence," from "Samuel W. Zimmer, 244 S. Sycamore Street, Petersburg, VA."

The doctor gave his nurse, Nellie, the $10 money order to log in the ledger and deposit it. She was accustomed to handling his notes and official business, after inheriting these duties from Dr. Lawrence's wife. Nellie had great attention to detail and kept things in perfect order.

Dr. Lawrence directed her to log the check, "Right there, next to that name, *Samuel Brant.*"

Puzzled, Nellie looked up at him and said "that's not the right line, sir." And she waited for his next answer.

He motioned with his index finger, saying "no, that's the same one, his real name is Zimmer, not Brant."

Nellie wrote the name "[*Zimmer*]" next to "Brant." And she did the same for all of the future checks that arrived. They all knew from that point forward that Zimmer was his real name.

Every single letter and check came from *"Sam'l Zimmer."* Every letter ended with the same unique abbreviated signature and distinguished handwriting. They were indicators of an educated man.

Dr. Lawrence, his wife, and Nellie discussed Sam's payment every time it arrived. Talk about when Sam would return for the baby gradually turned to conversations about *if* he would return. They talked about what to do with the baby girl. Mrs. Watson was asking for more financial help.

There was so much still undone and unknown. Complicating their ability to plan anything, Sam was not helping or communicating as one might expect a parent to do.

Days turned to weeks, weeks turned to months. Soon, it had been two years with no sight of Sam or Polly. It was clear now that they were done with this episode. All the while, Dr. Lawrence continued to treat the baby-turned-toddler, who remained healthy but for normal childhood ailments.

Every time he saw her, she was not only a baby he was treating, but she was the physical reminder of the strangest birth scene of his career. Her cherubic face was an attractive reminder to him of her prominent parentage. Ironically, her parentage was to her good fortune – her background compelled the doctor to protect her from a dark future in the black markets and orphanages and, instead, find her a good home where he believed her potential could be realized and protected.

Letters with Sam's checks continued to arrive for the first few months. Yet with each passing month, it became clear he and Polly wouldn't be coming back for the child anytime soon – or ever.

Sam Zimmer's political career was impressive, earning him a feature in a Who's Who Biography of Virginia. Sam Zimmer was: "Ambitious; University of Virginia Alumnus; Lawyer; Rapidly gained position; Virginia Legislator; Commonwealth's Attorney; Mayor." Beautiful, pedigreed wife, and father of two children.

Just one thing was missing. They left out the Zimmers' first-born daughter.

VIRGINIA BIOGRAPHY

Samuel Watts Zimmer, son of William Louis and Julia N. (Howland) Zimmer, was reared in Petersburg, receiving his education in the Episcopal High School of Virginia, and the University of Virginia, class of 1908. He was ambitious to become a lawyer, and studied to this end, and after his admission to the bar began practice in Petersburg, where he rapidly gained position, and in 1910 was elected a member of the Virginia legislature. In 1914 he became commonwealth's attorney of Petersburg, and in that position he is serving his constituency with credit and honor to himself and the satisfaction of the public. Ever since becoming a voter he has been a stanch supporter of the Democratic party, and exercises a large influence in its local councils. He is a member of Grace Protestant Episcopal Church of Petersburg, and follows the precepts of his honored father in furthering all efforts to advance the interests of the community. He married, January 4, 1909, Mary Blair Pryor Walker, daughter of Frank T. and Mary Blair (Pryor) Walker, granddaughter of General Roger A. Pryor, of New York, and his wife, Sarah Agnes (Rice) Pryor, and General R. Lindsay Walker and his wife, Maria Eskridge Walker. Mr. and Mrs. Zimmer are the parents of two children: Mary Blair Pryor and William Louis III.

She was not part of their public story. She was erased from Sam's public record and their sterling reputation. She was erased from Polly's mind, too.

The Secret Mary Blair

"What shall I put for a name on the birth certificate?" the doctor implored of Sam before leaving the boarding house with Sam's newborn.

"Just name her Mary Blair," Sam grumbled, signaling to the doctor his impatience. He was ready to leave at once.

As their secret baby was turning two years old just 100 miles away, they were celebrating Sam's second year as a Virginia legislator. Polly was busy planning her new baby's first birthday party in Petersburg.

Sam and Polly became established in Petersburg and had two recognized children, Mary Blair Pryor Zimmer in 1910 and William Louis III in 1912. At the same time, their secret daughter became known as Dorothy, the name given by her adoptive parents when they agreed to take her permanently from Dr. Lawrence.

Polly put the secret D.C. baby out of her mind. Did Sam tell her that the baby had died? That surely would have taken a great deal of mental effort and psychological denial to believe such a story. If, as a new mother, she genuinely believed her baby had died after childbirth, she would have formally buried it and memorialized it. If she planned to take the baby home to Petersburg and raise it, why would she hide her pregnancy by staying in D.C. for its duration?

If she thought the baby died, surely she would have mourned the baby. Surely, at a minimum, she would have claimed it as one of her official "live birth" counts on the U.S. Census in 1910. But she did neither. The baby was erased.

Polly must have made a deal with Sam to bury the secret. In exchange for not telling anyone in Petersburg about it, Sam was able to achieve ever-growing stature in the bustling town and the state, too. Together, they enjoyed a charmed life of privilege and power in Petersburg.

Polly obliged. She was complicit in holding tight the secret. Nobody, no one would ever drag it from her. The story of Polly's lost joy – the story of her quiet grief – would be hers alone forever to keep. She could not keep her baby nor mourn its loss without incurring the criticism of her high society peers. It was on her face, the shadow of sweet hopes denied, lovely visions unrealized.

Polly had dreams of sharing the beautiful antebellum home with Sam, and of curly-haired babies. She could have been numb with grief, but never shared it with him. She went about living. Did she experience a dull ache in her heart, robbed of the great sweetness of motherhood? Or did she bury it under her always-attractive exterior?

After a while, it would all fade away, Polly told herself. She would make herself forget. She refused to think about the baby. Yet, as summer arrived each year, she was reminded of the heat in the room when she delivered the secret baby. As the tree leaves changed and fell to the ground, her memory of that boarding room delivery faded, too.

Polly's recurrent dreams reminded her. In her nightmare, she saw Sam running down a long, narrow road. The road had thick, low bushes on each side of it, just as the South Sycamore Street home had. Sam was running after a little curly-haired girl, pursuing the child.

He was about to catch the child and kill her when Polly would hurl a hatchet at Sam, striking him the moment before he grasped the child's hair. Then, in a horror, Polly awoke each time from the nightmare.

Not only did she resent Sam for the child's extinguishing, but she could avenge the loss only in her dreams with a hatchet. Polly never blamed Sam for the loss of her child while awake; it was unspeakable and yet inevitable. She always awoke breathless with wonder at the freeing truths she found only in her dreams.

> *Judas bartered away his soul because, as a little boy, he saw his own mother sell her scarlet lips for gold.*
> J. Hay, Jr.

ERIN L. RICHMAN

7

Polly's Diary

1910, Petersburg

To the casual observer, my life may seem ruined, blasted beyond all hope. An early baby ruins many women. But to me, as long as I am capable of loving and as long as I have the love of even one person, it seems chastened, purified, endowed with even greater opportunities, more gorgeous duties, than I thought humanly possible.

The future? It is full of my husband's content. It has in it already the music of children's happy laughter. There are to be more children.

At first, I recoiled from that dream, thinking that a woman disgraced as I was by my ordeal had no right to bring into the world others who might share the results of her offenses. It is only by having children that I may make amends for what I did and what was done to me. There is only one way in which I can prevent my ignominy from doing me good. That would be by failing to take advantage of the lessons it has taught me.

The future, for me, is a field in which I shall find many flowers blooming — flowers for others as well as for myself.

1911, Thriving

I've taken the time on this last day of the year — New Year's Eve — to reflect with divine purpose. I am a firm advocate for the belief that we are authors for our own lives. So, by writing this and wishing for tranquility, serenity, and peace, I am hoping to will those sensations into my life in the forthcoming year. I want to focus on my baby Polly, our home life, gardening at our new home, bouncing my new baby, laughing with her, and just loving life with this angelic child.

I will never have these "Firsts" again. So, I wish to savor the moments with my precious babe as they come. Also, I pray that 1911 brings no new losses. I need a break from loss, please, Lord. I feel like life is being sucked out of me at the very time that I want to be feeling my most vibrant.

So, on this last day of the most unbelievable year, I ask for these things to come in abundance: peace, happiness, joy, fun, friendship, love, and, finally, both healing and financial abundance. That is my wish for 1911.

--

We are settled. We are blessed to have moved into a home we are in love with. We have left D.C. for good, settling next door to Sam's family. Sam's career is growing fast.

For our first time, we are on a stable upward course, happy with where we are, happy with what lies ahead, embracing any uncertainty as possibility. We are envisioning our future and we relish creating it.

Our home is not only on South Sycamore Street across from the park, but it feels like an actual park itself. From the cathedral ceilings, to the floor plan, to the porches, and the iron gates and the lawns, we love everything about it.

Today, I am breathless with gratitude as I contemplate the fact that Sam loves me and is boyishly happy in his realization that I love him as I do.

1912

Each day, I walk through the Petersburg sidewalks, I take in the smells of the rich Virginia soil, the beauty of our intricate gardens, and the tremendous pride of history in our hallowed halls.

I remind myself to never forget how much I had once longed for these trappings and vow to myself in my head to never take it for granted. It's an exercise in staying present in this lovely moment, and not getting lost in petty minutia that distracts us all from the things we truly love in our lives.

I love my child, my husband, my growing belly, and my growing family. I love my walks through beauty; divine music, and the inspiration I draw from others' life stories.

I have an abundance of these things right now and never want to forget how good it feels to savor them.

While a messy world filled with uncertainty swirls around me, I take comfort from the fact that my life is actually quite fulfilling, good, and insulated. I pray for the same for my sisters.

1917

My husband has failed me. Am I not utterly alone in all the world? I know now that I have been for a very long time exactly like hundreds of other women I have seen and known. They appear perfect, but are worn out, dissatisfied, miserable. To them, life has become barren, a tragedy. Yet, it appears to be in perfect, full bloom.

The flowers are all swept away, and there is left in their places only sham, make-believe, the paper blossoms that are without beauty and perfume. My face is companion to the faces of those women — it has the irritable look, the strained expression, the weary eyes, the perceptible tightness about the corners of the mouth, all badges of bitterness. Conflict within that I conceal.

There are times when I despise the thought of associating with anybody, when I shrink from the sound of others' voices, when I feel a hot scorn for everybody. These periods are followed by feverish days and nights when I try to pack the hours with every possible kind of amusement and distraction.

Instead of giving myself up to morbid thoughts and introspection, I throw myself into bridge, golf, the theater, dancing – but the enjoyment is ashes in my mouth, my laughter is always forced. I am trying to forget the misery caused by the knowledge of my husband's coldness, his lack of love.

Here we are, an endless parade of good-looking women, luxuriously housed, exquisitely gowned, elegantly groomed, sleek. This is what the world sees and envies.

But there is the other, real side of the picture – here we are, mourning in secret, weeping in the dark, starving for love, hungering for affection, reaching out futile hands for the dreams we shall never,

never realize, hiding our broken hearts under silks and pendants — hiding them from the world, but never from ourselves.

How full is the world of women trying to build up pathetic little palaces of happiness! There is left me only this despair, and with the despair come thoughts which I am afraid to admit even to myself.

Suffering pays visits that are frequent, visits that are long.

8

Three Sisters, Besieged

Polly's fourth baby was born on Jan 31st. Her pregnancy was uneventful, just has her other three pregnancies had been. She had made it through Christmas and New Year's festivities being very pregnant and very physically drained. So, she was ready for this baby to finally be born.

No one was prepared for the crisis that would come with the birth. The labor was normal. When the baby arrived, he was fully developed with ten fingers and ten toes. But his breathing was fast and his skin was a noticeable blue hue. The doctor knew something was wrong immediately. He quickly picked up the newborn and rushed out of the room.

Polly had been in this situation before, and the baby didn't come back. There was a feeling deeper than dread running through her veins, all over again.

This time, when the doctor returned, he explained that for the baby to survive outside his mother's womb, "he must have four fully-formed, fully-functioning chambers." All she could hear, ringing in her head over and over again,

"He was born with a heart that doesn't work."

The doctor told Polly he would not survive but maybe a day or two. Baby Sam Jr. died just two days after being born on February 2. They buried him the next day at Blandford Cemetery in his own plot.

The official cause of death was listed as *congenital heart failure*, which for most newborns, means being born with a heart not-fully-formed. Perhaps his vessel – his mother's body – couldn't complete him. Or, perhaps, the universe spared him from what might become a sad, tragic existence.

Polly wore a beautiful black veil at the quiet graveside service for her infant son, Samuel, Jr., that cold February morning. The soil was exposed, awaiting his tiny casket. The inner Earth would receive her sorrow; she need not show it on the surface. As the soil was tossed back into his tiny grave, it would shield his casket from the air, and shield Polly.

She wondered if she could carry on like this, even as everything appeared perfect on the surface. The picture of their life looked perfect, and *had to be* perfect. There was no oxygen for her to expel her grief.

Of course, people expressed their sorrow at her loss of new baby, Sam Jr. She was gracious in easing the sorrows others had burdened her with. She knew, of course, that losing a baby was the most difficult of life's losses. So, she tried staying inside the safety of the walls of her old brick home. Her trappings of perfection and accomplishment stifled any real connection or authentic happiness.

She felt a stifling silence, unable to grieve in her very public and beautiful life, and unable to admit to anyone the depth of her grief. She had not one, but, now, two babies taken from her. Four births, yet only two children.

Sam's election as *Mayor Zimmer* of Petersburg came soon after the death of their infant son. As his wife mourned the loss of her baby after bringing her pregnancy to full-term – *her second lost baby* – he was busy running for office, getting elected, and serving as mayor of the fine city.

Polly leaned on her two sisters, though she had it the easiest of the three of them, by comparison. She was the lucky one who married into wealth *and* status.

Yet, "lucky" isn't what she felt.

Her eldest sister, Lindsay, was newly divorced and raising her young daughter alone in Washington. Polly tried to help Lindsay as much as she could without troubling her with her own worries. After all, Polly *still* had her husband, so she kept her complaints to herself.

Polly had another older sister, Frances. Like Lindsay, Frances was also divorced. And, like Lindsay, she was struggling in Washington, emotionally and financially.

Frances' life was quite a disappointment for her. She watched as two of the closest women in her life – her sister, Polly, and her girlhood best friend, Nancy – ascended to the heights of society. Nancy, who had been Frances' lifelong friend from Virginia, became known around the world as *"Lady Astor."* Frances watched from afar as Nancy transformed into a legend, becoming the first woman ever to be elected to the British Parliament.

At the same time, Frances again watched from afar as her sister's husband was elected Mayor, and ran Petersburg's largest bank. It seemed everyone else was gaining wealth and stature, while she struggled.

Frances, now age 40, was increasingly frustrated and unfulfilled with her life. Plus, she was not doing well at raising her three children. Her 16-year-old daughter, Mary (named after her mother and sister), and 14-year-old son Lindsay still lived with her in Washington. Her eldest son, Dorsey, Jr., was 18 and had been removed from her care a few years before. Dorsey went to live with his grandparents (her ex-husband's parents) far away in rural Maryland. She had troubled relationships with each of her children.

Sadly, Frances had already lost a child, whose death rocked her young family. Her son's death was a shock to all when he died as a toddler at five years old. Little did they know then Frances' loss would be the first loss shared among the three Walker sisters.

As time would pass, Polly and Frances would share in common the loss of a child, something no two people wish to have in common, much less two sisters. Sharing their grief and dashed dreams might be the only thing Polly and Francis would have in common – something no two people wish to have in common, much less two sisters.

Dorsey knew his mother took her torments out on him. His mother hit Dorsey brutally on many occasions, and, naturally, he resented her intensely. No one could blame him. Frances was explosive, and still very hostile toward Dorsey's father, her ex-husband. Dorsey was a scarred young man, and whenever he spoke about his mother, his anguish was like an open wound.

To survive, Dorsey avoided his mother Frances, as their volatile relationship only became more strained after his parents' divorce. Though Dorsey distanced himself from his mother, he still kept in contact with his Aunt Lindsay. Lindsay helped him land a good job working for the census bureau, so he was able to get some stability. He was doing well on his own, especially now as an independent 18-year-old.

Life marched on for Polly – if effortfully – in Petersburg, though she did not share her struggles with anyone. Her sisters were both barely hanging on themselves. As Polly remained atop the Petersburg social scene, ever-beautiful and perfect, she remained the envy for her outer "attractiveness." Her inner woes were not exposed, nor would they ever be – not to her sisters, not to her friends, not to her husband, no one.

She swallowed her woes whole that February.

9

--
February's Woe

    Polly's phone rang in the middle of a cold February night in 1925. Polly recognized the frantic voice on the phone as her sister, Lindsay's. She struggled to keep herself calm.

    "Polly!" Lindsay shouted in what seemed like unending, howling syllables through sobs on the telephone.

    "Lindsay! What is it my dear! What is wrong!?" Polly begged.

Lindsay could not speak. She could only sob. And howl. She tried to get it out, to get the horrific words out.

The police had found a letter in Frances' apartment in Washington, steps away from three deceased bodies in a gas-filled apartment in D.C.

The letter was written by Frances. And her letter was a farewell, addressed to her two sisters,

"*Dear Lindsay and Polly*"... she wrote.

"*I am tired of struggling and being unhappy and being poor..*"

"*This is far better than anything else I've ever done,*"

She closed the letter.

Frances' farewell letter was sitting on the kitchen counter in her Washington apartment, just steps from her dead body, and those of her two children. Her son Lindsay was 14 and her daughter Mary 16. This mother had not only killed herself, but also two of her three living children.

Like his Aunt Polly, Dorsey Jr. learned from Lindsay, too, that his mother killed herself and his only siblings. Frances' son, Dorsey Jr. was the lucky one. He was lucky to have been removed five years earlier. As a young man of 21 years, he would live the rest of his life knowing his mother killed his brother and sister. Dorsey's scars became deep and unspeakable.

Wealth and abundant opportunity – tasted by all of the Walker-Pryor grandchildren – had passed by Dorsey's mother, Frances. Wealth and opportunity abounded in 1925, but not for Frances.

Frances Walker Waters, Washington, kills self and two children, read the headline the next day. She killed her children and herself with gas from the kitchen stove.

The month of February, Polly's birthday month, would now be forever be the month her infant son died, and the month her sister killed herself and two of her children. Her birthday would never be the same again.

Sam would eventually ascend as the President of Ashland Railway Company. At the same time, he was President of the Petersburg Savings and American Trust Company. In the 1927 Petersburg City Directory, the company proudly boasted "Total Resources, $6,000,000" in its advertisements.

"STRENGTH MEANS SAFETY"

"Safety," Sam's company's ad promised. He led them through unprecedented growth and profits in the 1920's boom years.

Little did they know what peril awaited in the coming years.

Polly's slide, 1928

Polly lived a life feeling like "my body failed me *again*."

Sam remained an absent husband and Polly had her two young children to care for, all while she maintained the role of Mayor's wife among Petersburg's social set. To make matters worse, she went through bouts with her migraines, shutting herself in for days on end.

Polly's sights slowly became grimmer.

"Sometimes the best option feels like escape," she'd say to Lindsay in the grand parlor of 244 South Sycamore. As before, Lindsay knew her sister's grief, physical and spiritual. Lindsay could only offer her the comfort of her visits.

"I am not sure if it's me or if it's my marriage. Or if it's being 40. Or if it's being bored," Polly explained.

Sam had little empathy for her melancholy or migraines. He swept swiftly past the infant's death, and continued his political work. To Polly, his silence after the baby died was deafening.

Sam was an intelligent man. Surely, he could see the irony. His first whiff of his feelings was a combined, twisted relief, mixed with stark horror that the sin of that surrendered, secret D.C. baby had just come full circle in the form of a dead baby. Horror. Yet culpability. He didn't plan this part. So, he upheld the pretense that all was well and threw himself into his work.

Maybe he could plant seeds in Polly's head in such a way that she would just blame herself for being defective at carrying babies.

"Maybe it is just not your destiny to have a house full of children, Polly," he said to her once, as if their first baby's absence was somehow fate.

As her melancholy grew, he became exasperated at the real possibility that she might not recover this time. His goal was to get her to snap out of it. He tried many things. He took them both on a cruise to Europe.

Polly's migraines only grew worse, and her withdrawals from the world became more frequent. He was no consolation to her, as his compassion was no salve.

"When will you be ready to leave the house again?" he prodded, letting Polly know that her unattractive attitude was challenging to his social commitments. In her inner translation, all she heard from him was 'why couldn't she just get happier?'

"You have two perfectly healthy and beautiful children. You have this life. What more could you possibly want?" Sam said, as if her gratitude for her children would displace the loss of two others.

She found him of no consolation.

Successful, popular lawyer. Beautiful wife, pedigreed Pryor and Zimmer names. Security, status. Why wasn't it enough for her?

Polly saw the burning, assured looks he gave to other women in Petersburg. She saw him hold glances with women, interlocked as if by physical means, at social affairs. She saw the hungry look in other women's eyes as they looked at Sam. She knew this, and, yet, Sam was the most interesting man she had ever encountered.

Everyone said to her, every day, "Polly, what a charming husband you have!" Men as well as women admired Sam. He was attractive in every aspect of the word.

Yet Sam was a man who used up away from home so much of his likability, pleasantness, and affection, that he had very little left for his wife. At home, he was tired, drifting along, giving little.

Sam was handsome, rich, and powerful. This son of a tobacco king had the wind at his back and a promising future. His father groomed him and his brother, William, to be ready to carry on the family name, and take it to greater heights.

Having a wife at home who was miserably ill dragged him down. His patience was thin, and yet his ambition was kept its stride.

Polly felt guilty for not being a *good, cheerful* Southern wife – as described by grandmother Sara Pryor in her book of etiquette. Sara was a towering figure, yet none of her grandchildren would come near meeting her legacy.

Her sister Frances' words in her suicide note still rang in her head. Frances' tragic final written words were that her act of murder-suicide was *'far better than anything else I've ever done.'* Polly wondered if perhaps the same could be true for her, too. Polly's unshakable grief was breaking her. Her pain was physically inescapable.

Sam's distance did not help. Polly needed more. Yet, she struggled with guilt for not living up to 'good wife' expectations.

Polly's mind was a cobweb of desperation and sadness. Her life – attractive to those in Petersburg unaware of the secrets from Washington – seemed a picture of vacuous perfection.

The roaring 20's did not roar happily for Polly, and she went further inward and downward as the years advanced.

Her well ran dry. Others have won battles like hers and persisted. Polly lost. Losing two babies was too much for one soul to bear. They told everyone it was her migraines, and an accidental overdose of her medication. Her melancholy and grief were forever shrouded in secret.

By early 1930, the advertisements in the City Directory were cut in half. There was no trace of the Petersburg Savings and American Trust Company. Strength didn't mean safety for anyone.

After the stock market crash in Fall 1929, time stood still for most Americans. The adult generation in Virginia who had been raised to preserve "Old Virginia" had no room for this depression. People were simply emotionally stranded, wondering how to make sense of *The Great Depression*. Few had skills to cope. Disorder and chaos became the norm.

"I'll be a rainbow and shine down on my mother.
Sharp knife of a short life.
Who would've thought forever could be severed by
the sharp knife of a short life?"
                                                       - *Kimberly Perry*

ERIN L. RICHMAN

Polly's Ode to Sam – June, 1928

We started so grand, our wedding filled that house made of brick
    You had captivated my mind and so filled my womb

    However, could anyone – let alone me – predict
Our secret would plummet to that dirty boarding room…

Yes, how I believed you that our first was born; then died?
    Yours were loyalties even my sister would own.

    I held fiercely our best hopes even amidst cries.
Details – no matter. Your light still so brightly shone.

Death's angels reach out at me, ever-taunting me all these years,
    First one baby, then another; and my sister too – oh, Christ!

Parading my smile nonetheless amidst the crowds and cheers.
Your ambitions left no room, so I shut in with my dark eyes.

It makes sense in this wicked life that we all take our turn –
    So, my fate is now – to meet death's angels' burn.

OF MARY BLAIR DESTINY

10

--
Gladly

"*I am a nurse by profession. I was formerly assistant to Dr. Albert L. Lawrence, physician.*

I remember, because of the developments, the case of the birth of the child called "Mary Blair."

It was the custom of Dr. Lawrence to talk with me about his cases, a custom which is natural and usual between physician and nurse.

I knew, of course, of the birth; prepared his bag for him when he went to attend it. I knew, of course, the place of birth; and I knew of the birth return.

A week after the baby was born, Dr. Lawrence told me of the circumstances surrounding the birth. He told me about the parents, their social positions, etc. He told me the father's name, Mr. Samuel Zimmer, and his place of residence, Petersburg, Virginia. He said the Mother was a very pretty young woman. He told me the father was in great distress of mind because of the situation; was fearful of his family if the matter became known; that he never saw a man more excited in such a case. Sam said they could not take the baby home with them and it would have to be put in some one care for a while; that later they were going West to settle and then they would go by way of Washington and get the baby.

He told me the father insisted the mother should not see the baby, and that though, he, the doctor, had tried to get the baby in to the mother, the father had insisted he should not and prevented it; that the baby had been taken to Mrs. Watson without the Mother seeing it.

In the letters which Sam wrote to the doctor on the occasions of sending the money orders, he more than once showed a distressed mind over the possibility of discovery of the matter by his family, speaking of his fears in that respect. In one of his letters, he said he did not see how he would ever be able to take the child.

Later on in his letters, Sam, in addition to his complaining about his condition financially making it difficult to give the small amount agreed for the keep of the child, referred to the fact that his financial ability would still be further crippled by another child to be born to his wife. Finally, he not only refused to pay any more, but stopped sending money altogether, and he was two or three months behind when Dr. Lawrence found a home for the *baby. Dr. Lawrence was greatly worried about the situation and did not know what to do with the baby. "*

Nellie J. Wilson, nurse to Dr. Albert Lawrence

Summer, 1911

Nellie Wilson knew the whole story. She had been the one to open the doctor's mail, and log Sam Zimmer's money orders and his letters. She read Sam's words of worry over his secret being revealed to his family, especially his father. She read his words of distress with her own eyes; she saw his refusal to pay for more support.

Nellie was there to listen as the doctor often worried aloud about what to do with the baby. She encouraged him to persist in caring for the baby and finding her a permanent home. No legal obligation bound him to do so, yet, luckily for her sake, he did the right thing.

Days turned to weeks, weeks turned to months. Months would quickly turn to years. And the time was quickly coming that the baby would begin talking and asking questions.

Soon, two full years passed since the baby was born and "returned" to the doctor by the mysterious Sam and beautiful Polly of Petersburg. Sam finally saw a way out of it all completely. A way to wash his hands forever from this baby, from the lie, from the payment, from any trace of it.

The baby, Mary Blair, was passed around to whomever was willing to take care of it for the $10 a month the doctor promised. Sam was supposed to send the doctor a monthly $10 to cover the baby's expenses, but, on several occasions, he had fallen several months behind.

How could this be?

Sam had plenty of money to spare. The truth, however, was that no amount of money would fill the empty void of feeling or care for this baby. He had zero intrinsic interest and no intent to ever reclaim her.

She was a problem they wished to dispose of, not a child they wished to raise.

The lie had now been cemented. The $10 per month were simply dues to keep it hidden. As long as Sam paid the fee, the baby and the horrific lies to hide her lived on, undetectable.

Eventually, the dues went unpaid. Serving as a state representative to the House of Delegates, and working as the Commonwealth's attorney, Sam bemoaned his strained financial situation to Dr. Lawrence. The simple fact was, Sam begrudged sending the money.

Dr. Lawrence was worried. He was tired of tracking Sam down for the $10 every month. Mrs. Watson showed distress to the doctor, expressing that she could not afford care anymore for the almost-2-year-old without more money. She needed at least $15.

Dr. Lawrence wrote to Sam asking for more support for the baby's basic needs. Sam said no. He explained, not only would he not be providing additional monthly dollars, but he said he would not continue to pay $10 – the amount he had originally committed to when he left the baby two years before.

Dr. Lawrence finally grasped reality. Sam was never going to come get his baby. He figured out that Sam would stop supporting the baby now, too.

This ordeal became Dr. Lawrence's to resolve.

The baby needed a home and the doctor needed to wash his hands of the unwanted commitment. Dr. Lawrence was ready to be done with managing it. The question was, who would be willing to take this baby on a permanent basis?

Dr. Lawrence had been asking around, and he thought he might have a couple interested.

Dr. Lawrence wrote to Sam, telling him of the chance to get a good home for the child and asking him if he agreed to never claim the child.

Sam wrote back: "Gladly," he would comply with this request.

Gladly.

Sam was ready to be done with this baby. He didn't care who it would be given to – he didn't want to know. He had no questions about the family's standing. No questions about their ability to raise a child. No questions about the setting in which the child would be raised, much less the city.

Clearly, Sam never intended to be part of this child's life – not now, not ever. He wanted her out of their life for good.

Meanwhile, Bertha and George Hardy wondered if they should take in the baby that they had heard needed a home.

Bertha Hardy had long ago given up on having children from her own body. She and George were never so lucky to have a baby naturally. So, when George came home talking about a baby girl in the care of their friends, the Rileys, Bertha nodded half-listening.

"The baby needs a home, Bertha. What do you think?" George sheepishly asked his wife.

She thought he was crazy. She dismissed the idea without second thought.

Flatly, she told him, "No."

In any case, she thought to herself, if he was serious about this, he would come back to her and need to convince her.

When he did, she did not expect to be so compelled. Mrs. Riley had talked glowingly of this active, attractive baby to Bertha's sister, Lily. Mrs. Riley knew the baby well. She took the baby in her home as a favor to Dr. Lawrence after Mrs. Watson could no longer support it.

Mrs. Riley was intent on finding her a good home. She thought the baby deserved a good home, as she directly saw how happy, bright, and cute the baby was. She wanted to find someone to love this baby and preserve her chances for a good life.

Lily relayed the story as she heard it from Mrs. Riley: The baby was left behind right after she was born. She had been orphaned by a prominent Virginia family who needed to maintain appearances because she was born "too early" for their marriage.

The Rileys had questions about her legitimacy, but also had an urgency to find her a home, as she had been being passed around for nearly two years. Mrs. Watson could no longer afford to take her back into her care. Dr. Lawrence knew the situation had become untenable. He wanted to resolve this and find the baby a permanent home.

George convinced Bertha to consider it. She still was on the fence.

Finally, in late summer, August, 1911, Bertha drove up from Indian Head, Maryland, to visit her sister Lily Stuart in D.C. Lily wanted to show the baby to Bertha, and let Bertha see for herself in person how the baby needed a home. Lily fully dressed and cleaned up the baby. Dr. Lawrence had recently placed a cast on the baby's arm after a fall from a swing broke it. Bertha would see her cherubic face and blonde baby hair for herself. The cast, if not the cherub cheeks, would break Bertha.

Lily knew what to do and what to say to her sister to help her come to this fateful decision. Bertha Hardy melted like butter. In Bertha's own words:

> "After seeing her, I said I would take her and she remained with us, in my care, from then on. I intended to raise her as my own, birth certificate did not matter, though Dr. Lawrence offered to take Mr. Hardy to Health Office to show record of birth, as well

> to Petersburg; no one claimed her; did not want her to retain any recollections that might open up any unpleasant recollections of the 'unfortunate circumstances in which she was left;' told Father Hann all about the child's birth; her Baptism at St. Ignatius Roman Catholic Church."

Bertha took Polly's baby home, and renamed her new daughter Dorothy. She loved the baby as her own, raising her as her own.

Bertha became "Mother B" to the baby *she chose*. Innocently, Dorothy herself had affectionately coined "Mother B." The nickname stuck with Bertha even as grandmother to Dorothy's future children.

At last, Bertha's child was Dorothy, the energetic and intelligent and attractive child.

She was a child who got her very own pony for her 4th birthday.

She was a child to whom adults took the time to explain things. Dorothy was the Hardys' sole focus, getting their complete attention. As older adults, they were wiser than typical parents. They had many experiences to share with their unexpected and beloved daughter.

Dorothy learned to play piano, so well she later gave lessons herself. Dorothy was beloved not by her parents alone, but also by her only aunt and uncle, Lily and George. They had to be shared with no one, for there were no other siblings or cousins in their little family.

Dorothy, alone, was the child upon whom they spent their money, sent to private boarding school, and provided support for extra business training. By fateful coincidence, Dorothy and Sara Pryor shared in common their condition of being informally adopted, enriched and loved as only children.

Dorothy was loved. She was doted upon and encouraged to excel in school. She was raised with a profound, reverent, and dutiful Catholic faith. She grew into a person who obeyed rules, even if she was an unknowing product of breaking them.

ERIN L. RICHMAN

The Hardys had a daughter of their own – *gladly*.

Sam's Self-Defense

I had other plans, you see

I could taste the precipice of my own success, savor it, for me.

Beautiful wife and joint ambitions elevated us both quickly

Taking an early baby home would have meant we would lose more than our dignity – and dearly.

We would have had no life; for, with us, she could never be.

Leaving the baby at least saved the beautiful wife and me.

And our future children's lives? My leaving her behind saved them plenty.

Sure, I left a baby, abandoned, but at least she was free.

She was free from the stuffy confines of our high society.

Sure, she didn't stand a chance, though her welfare didn't concern me.

I gave her freedom; she was free from me.

She was free from her mother's melancholy.

She was free from invisible costs of our preserved dignity.

My other plans for us ended abruptly and early.

I tasted great success for myself, surely.

But in the end, if I am honest (which I try not to be), her abandoned life shone the most brilliantly.

I gave her freedom, and, well, quite excellent heredity.

For that and her abandonment, she can thank me.

11

--
Fast Forward: 1931

Dorothy had recently discovered her real birth story after a strange turn of events during her pursuit of a career with the U.S. government. The hiring process became fateful for Dorothy, as it required a search for her birth certificate.

It had been two months since Dorothy first asked her mother for her birth certificate as part of her job search. Dorothy accepted the explanation, though she aptly noticed that something had been eating at her mother.

Indeed, her instincts were right. Mother B had been fretting over what to tell Dorothy. She had been raising Dorothy all these years as her own daughter, never addressing the fact that she was not her biological daughter. There was no easy way to reveal the secret, but Bertha knew now was the time.

She decided to tell Dorothy on that Sunday night in June, 1931. Her birthday was a few days away, and it would never be the same.

But what Bertha could not tell Dorothy was what she *did not* know about her natural parents. She knew only a few facts. They were well-heeled, from Virginia, and they left her immediately when she was born in the care of Dr. Lawrence. They had the last name Zimmer.

"When you asked me for your birth certificate, I knew the time had come," Bertha began.

"Since that day in March, I have been gathering more than just your birth certificate. I don't know where to begin, my dear, other than with the facts. Your birth certificate was not in Baltimore, as you were not born in Maryland, but in Washington D.C."

"Okay," Dorothy exhaled with a hint of confusion, unsure why Mother B was so serious in her tone to deliver the simple news that she was not born in Maryland but in D.C.

Mother B continued, "Dorothy, none of what I am about to share changes that you are my child and forever will be. I love you as my child."

Dorothy sat quietly, her eyes fixed on Mother B and waiting for what seemed like more to come. The moment was incredibly perplexing.

"Dorothy, you were born in D.C. to a woman and man who were from Virginia. They were married, but we got you because they could not take you home with them, as you were born too early for their marriage," Bertha spoke carefully and steadily.

"Daddy and I are not your natural parents. We got you when you were a baby and have loved and raised you as our own because you have been nothing but our daughter to us," her voice accentuating her sincerity and weight of the news.

"After you asked me for your birth certificate, I decided to contact to the doctor's office who originally gave you to us. Dr. Lawrence, the doctor who delivered you, died years ago, but his wife and his nurse are still around. I have talked with them, and they helped me locate your official birth certificate at the Office of Vital Statistics. They remember you very well and how beautiful of a baby you were," Bertha said, laying bare the basic facts.

Transcript No. 7540

Record No. 158,312

HEALTH DEPARTMENT, DISTRICT OF COLUMBIA

TRANSCRIPT FROM THE RECORD OF BIRTHS

REPORT OF A BIRTH

Use this form ONLY in case the child BREATHES or shows other evidence of LIFE after the child is altogether outside the mother's body; in other cases use the form provided for the reporting of STILLBIRTHS. If a stillbirth occurs in the practice of a midwife she must report it IMMEDIATELY to the Coroner. This may be done through the nearest police station.

Place of birth ___211 C St., N. W.___
(Give Street and Number)

Full name of child ___MARY BLAIR BRANT___
(If not named when this report is made, parents should make supplemental report)

Sex of child ___Female___ Twins? _____ Triplets? _____

If more than one child was born, state whether this report refers to the first, second, or third, etc.

Date of birth ___Wednesday, June 2, 1909___

* Legitimate? ~~Yes~~ ~~No~~ ~~Unknown~~

FATHER	MOTHER
Full name ___Samuel Brant___	Maiden name ___Mary Blair___
Residence ___Richmond, Va.___	Residence ___Richmond, Va.___
Color ___White___ Age at last birthday ___25___ yrs.	Color ___White___ Age at last birthday ___21___ yrs.
Birthplace ___Va.___	Birthplace ___Va.___
Occupation ___Solicitor___	Occupation ___Housewife___

Number of children born to this mother, including present birth ___1___
Number of children of this mother now living ___1___

CERTIFICATE OF ATTENDING PHYSICIAN OR MIDWIFE

I HEREBY CERTIFY that I attended at the birth of this child, and that it occurred on the ___2nd___ day of ___June___, 19___09___, at ___5___ P. m., and that the above information in so far as not based upon my personal observation was furnished by ___Father___, whose relationship to this child is that of ___above___, and whose address is ___211 C St., N. W.___

Signature of ___Albert L. Lawrence, M. D.___
(Physician or midwife)

Dated ___June 5, 1909___ Address ___1102 L St., N. W.___

Given name _____ added from supplemental report _____ 19___
*A child is legitimate if either conceived or born in wedlock.

REMARKS: _____

Correct mgdp/ _____ WASHINGTON, D. C., ___June 27th, 1931___

The foregoing is a true and correct copy of a certificate of birth filed with the Health Department of the District of Columbia on ___June 10th___, 19___09___, and duly recorded in the records of said Department.

_____ M. D.

At the age of 21, Dorothy was jolted learning that Mother B and Daddy were not, in fact, her natural parents and she was "adopted." Her birth certificate sat on the coffee table in front of her, right next to the only Mother she had ever known, yet now knew she was not her birth mother. The official piece of paper sat there on the coffee table – flat, pale and lifeless – looking just as Dorothy's face looked in that moment.

Telling Dorothy the truth was not easy. Bertha had no script for what to tell your adult daughter when she learns she's adopted and was given up at birth. Bertha could instantly see that these revelations upset Dorothy, despite her tempered comportment.

In fact, she was never even adopted legally. Mother and Daddy had no legal parentage, making them her "foster parents." Moreover, she was shocked to learn that her natural parents were affluent Virginians who gave her up because she was born "too early" for what was considered proper.

Her daughter's life was moving along swimmingly until now, but Bertha knew telling the truth was the right thing to do, even if it was painful. She and Dorothy decided together that they would go down the path to find out more about her biological parents.

Mother B encouraged Dorothy to investigate so they could determine the exact facts, unsure where it might lead but resolute it was the right thing to do. She was guided by her love for Dorothy and the desire to see her at peace with this revelation. In Bertha's own words:

"Solely out of my love and affection for her, and for such preservation and use by her as she may desire and see fit to make.

To us, she remains our child as she has always been."

"I have been down to Petersburg once already with Daddy since March. I've been to D.C. to get your records, but there is probably more you will want to know. Tomorrow, when you get to work at the Census, you should look up all the Census records you can find for Petersburg and for the name Zimmer."

Dorothy went to work the next day and followed her mother's direction.

First thing that morning, she went to see the clerk in charge of these Virginia records at the Census office, who was housed in her very same building. Dorothy entered the office, not sure what she was about to find, but she strode confidently into the office determined to find answers about her parents and whoever else might be connected to them.

As luck would have it, the clerk was not there, but one of his assistants was there in his absence. The assistant was none other than Mr. Herbert D. Waters. Mr. Waters was someone Dorothy had never seen in the building before, and he was no more than a stranger to her. He seemed friendly enough, yet she was still nervous navigating this unexpected path.

Only 12 hours earlier, she learned she was not the natural daughter of the only two people she had ever known as her parents. Here she was, standing in a census clerk's office in her very place of employment, seeking information on her birth parents. It was all too much.

Little did she know where this encounter might lead. She gathered herself in one breath and asked the question.

"Good morning, I would like to speak to the clerk. Is he in today?" Dorothy asked the assistant, who was perched behind a desk.

"Well, no, ma'am, I'm sorry, he is not. May I help with something?" the assistant asked.

"I am here looking for records for Petersburg, Virginia. Do you know what records the clerk might have on Petersburg?" Dorothy asked, focused on her task and not on the assistant's friendliness.

"I don't know, ma'am. I am not sure what he has."

Quickly shifting gears, the clerk, Mr. Waters, eagerly asked, "But have you ever heard of Mr. Sam Zimmer of Petersburg?"

"No, I have not," Dorothy quickly answered, confused by the question-as-an-answer to her question.

He continued, "Mr. Zimmer married my aunt, Miss Polly Walker, who was the sister of my mother, Frances. My mother is now dead, though. And so is my aunt."

What had just happened was stranger than fiction. This man – the assistant standing in for the Virginia clerk that Monday morning in June – was Herbert D. Waters. He looked to be about her same age. The "D." – his middle initial – stood for Dorsey. Dorsey was the name he was called by friends and family. He was Dorothy's first cousin.

This man was standing before Dorothy, and uttering the very same last name to her that she had heard hours before.

In fact, her mother had just spoken the name "Zimmer" the previous night when telling Dorothy "the news."

"I am so very sorry for your loss. That is horrible, I best get back to my desk," Dorothy replied, unsure what to say next and confused about what was happening. "Thank you for your time. Have a good day," Dorothy turned and quickly walked out.

As she entered the stairwell, she stopped. She took a moment to gather herself and double check with herself what she had just heard. She stood there, looking down, while holding the stair rail, mouthing to herself, "Zimmer?" In her head, she asked herself if it was possible that the young assistant actually just uttered that name. Did he really just say that?

She went back up to her desk and sat down for a moment before getting back up to hunt down a Petersburg phone directory. She wanted to look up the name Zimmer in the Petersburg phone book and narrow down the possible names of her birth parents.

The phone directories for the Maryland-Virginia-Delaware areas were all stored on the same shelf in the large supply closet on her floor. Her 5'2" frame could barely reach the top shelf.

She got a stool, placed it firmly in front of the cabinet, and stepped up. She reached her arms above her head, thumbing through the various Virginia cities that were lined up on the shelf. And, finally, she spotted it, grabbing the thin directory for Petersburg.

Dorothy stepped down from the stool, holding this directory in her hands, and walked back over to her desk. She sat down before opening it, restraining herself from looking. In her chair now, she leaned forward and opened the directory. Her first research discovery awaited.

She saw the names of companies, people, and shops. She turned the pages slowly. Studying each line, she saw Petersburg people and businesses listed in these pages. She flipped.

Then, toward the end of the directory, at the top of the page, she unknowingly read Sam's ad,

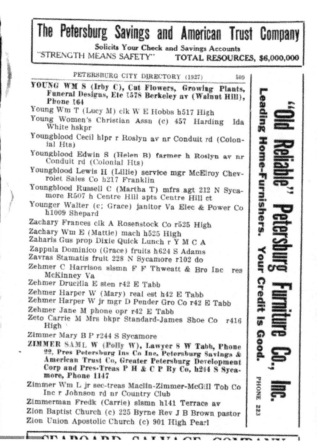

**Petersburg Savings and American Trust Company
Total Resources, $6,000,000"
"STRENGTH MEANS SAFETY"**

Finally, underneath the advertisement, nearing the end of the book, she saw the names starting with the letter Y, knowing Z was coming at any line. Her eyes moved slowly down the page.

One line stood out amongst every other name on the page.

ZIMMER, SAML W. (Polly W.) Lawyer

Was this him – Dorothy's father?

Surely, it could not be the same person that the man Dorsey had just mentioned downstairs. There were three Zimmer entries. One was an unmarried female, leaving just two possibilities.

She stood straight up, grasping the directory, and headed back to Dorsey's office. She showed him the directory. Dorsey noticed her possessing more intensity than she had on her initial visit a few minutes earlier. She clearly was on a mission Dorsey correctly realized.

"Hello, again. Would you kindly look at this? This is the Petersburg directory I just found. Do you know these men, Samuel and William Zimmer?" the words came out of Dorothy's mouth like a lawyer in cross-examination.

"Yes, I do! Sam is the one who married my Aunt Polly, the sister of my dead mother, Frances. They're all dead," Dorsey recounted in his matter-of-fact, half-funny way.

Not knowing who he was speaking to, Dorsey accepted death and was not afraid to talk about it plainly, especially since his mother and siblings' deaths. A "particular sort of cuss," Dorsey did not care much for avoiding taboo.

"Sam was killed when he stepped in front of an automobile a couple weeks ago... so shocking still. Polly died of an overdose a few years ago. Such a shame, my cousins were basically orphaned," his voice trailed off solemnly.

Little did he know the irony of which he spoke.

"Cousins?" Dorothy responded with surprise.

"Yes, they had two kids, one daughter and one son. They are my cousins. They live there still at that address on South Sycamore," Dorsey explained, pointing at the address.

Dorothy's birth certificate named her parents as Samuel W. and Mary Blair, yet the names in the directory were "*Saml* and *Polly W.*" These could not be the same people, yet so much else was a match: Samuel, Zimmer, lawyer. Those were the details Mother B shared. How many Samuel Zimmer lawyers could there be in Petersburg? She was baffled.

Maybe this was her father and he was now with another woman?

"There is no way my two could still be married," she said, thinking aloud.

"Plus, this woman's name is Polly. My mother was Mary Blair. It cannot be the same person," she continued to utter out loud, as if Dorsey was not even there.

"Actually, Polly is just a nickname for Mary Blair. We call all the Mary Blair's Polly, even my grandmother," Dorsey interjected without being asked.

Saml W. and Polly were, in fact, Samuel and Mary Blair. This must be the two listed on Dorothy's birth certificate.

But, certainly, there was no way they had two children. If they were her parents, they would not be married, and definitely would not have other children... since they gave *her* away?

In actuality, during the previous 12 hours since learning of her birth story from Bertha, Dorothy assumed – wrongly – her parents gave her away because they were not married. They were married because of the pregnancy, but she was given away because she was too early for their social standards. It would have been evident to everyone in Petersburg that Sam and Polly conceived this baby out of wedlock with her birth occurring just five months after their wedding. Why did Sam marry Polly when she became pregnant if they would just give the baby away?

If this "*Saml and Polly*" were indeed her parents, then they not only went back to Petersburg after she was born, but they remained married and also had more children. If these were her parents, then she was the daughter of Samuel and Polly Zimmer, who lived at 244 S. Sycamore Street. If these were her parents, they were now dead.

If these were indeed her parents, then not only was she adopted, but she also had a sister and a brother. A full sister. A full brother.

If these were her parents, then Dorsey, the man standing in front of her at this very desk in the Census Bureau, was – her cousin?

Less than 12 hours after learning she was adopted, was she now looking in the eyes of a blood relative and someone who knew her parents? And her sister and brother? She was indeed.

"May I sit down for a moment?" Dorothy requested of Dorsey, trying to comprehend this moment.

"Of course, have a seat. Why is it you are looking for the Zimmers?" he asked of Dorothy.

Still fresh from the shock of the previous evening's news, she spoke the words, still stranger to her than fiction, "I believe they may be my parents. Their names are listed on my birth certificate. If it is them, they gave me away after I was born in D.C. I just learned this all myself last night," she said seeking relief in the eyes of this stranger and holding her head.

This Monday morning was like no other in Dorothy's 21 years. And her life would never be the same from this moment forward. What started out as a search for a birth certificate to get a new job turned into a journey of discovery.

She could have never imagined that her steps into the Board of Education just three months earlier would lead to all of this.

She and Dorsey looked at each other, listening intently, while studying each other's faces for anything familiar. He noticed how much she resembled her father. "Dorothy is a spitting image of Uncle Sam," he thought to himself.

Dorsey heard her story, listening in wonder, and immediately enjoyed bonding with this stranger. Before they knew it, it was nearly lunchtime. Nearly two hours had passed.

He shared that he still had still one surviving aunt in Washington. His Aunt Lindsay Walker Hay was the only aunt remaining from his mother's side, and they still spoke to each other regularly. Dorsey offered to introduce Dorothy to Lindsay, the woman who they both could now refer to as an aunt.

Aunt Lindsay was divorced, working for the FBI in the Department of Justice building just a few blocks away at 10th and Pennsylvania. She lived in an apartment just across the Potomac with her elderly mother, Polly Walker. Dorsey wanted the two to meet, as he assumed Lindsay would love to meet a long-lost niece.

By a strange twist of fate, Dorothy crossed paths with Dorsey Waters at work in Washington D.C. It was incredible that he was her first cousin, something she would not know immediately, but was nonetheless quickly revealed to her.

Dorsey and Dorothy: full-blood, first cousins, and, now, friends.

OF MARY BLAIR DESTINY

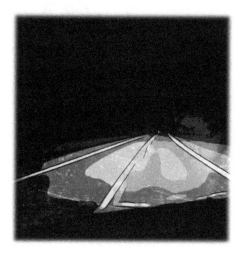

12

--
1931: Dorothy Digs for Truth

"A woman visited here yesterday asking questions to uncover the details of the secret baby ordeal. She knows many details about it. She asked for the birth certificate, and she asked for your real names. She appeared to already know the story, the true story, and is busy tracking down proof," the letter to Sam read.

Dorsey said that, in April or May 1931, Sam may have gotten advance word from associates – possibly Lindsay Walker Hay, possibly the widow of Dr. Lawrence – that someone was asking questions about the 1909 baby. A woman was asking questions about a birth certificate, a Dr. Lawrence, and a baby born in D.C.

Sam knew the story; he was its author. The only other person who knew of the secret baby was Polly, and she was buried six feet under by this point. Lindsay had kept this secret for Sam for all these years, even after her sisters' suicides. His biography remained sterling despite his secret flagrancies. He knew trouble was coming.

What may have struck him was that she had Sam's real name, Zimmer. This woman had his dark secret – *THE* scandal. She had the birth certificate.

Perhaps what might have struck him more than anything else – this mystery woman had the doctor's records of his payments and his letters.

"And this woman said she would be going to Petersburg soon to gather even more of the truth," the letter said.

How could it be that anyone who was alive knew? Sam long ago thought this was done and gone for good. He had certainly put it out of his mind two decades ago quickly after his last payment to Dr. Lawrence. The baby didn't even happen in his mind, and he convinced Polly of the same.

If this first lie was revealed, what else of Sam's frauds might also be revealed?

Bertha's initial facts gave Dorothy a good start, but she still had so many questions. She began a quest for anything at all that might corroborate what Dorsey had told her. Nothing made sense.

She felt the life she understood had been blasted to bits. The unpretentious yet ambitious path she had been creating for herself imploded instantly.

Dorothy wanted to know more – her parents, their stories, why. How could they have given her away and stayed married? Did they know about her at all now? Did they even want to? What did they look like? Who did she look like?

Mother B, fraught with worry for her daughter's mental well-being, wanted to do something, too. She knew only scant details and had more questions than answers about this family. Her daughter's clandestine birth was of no matter to Bertha. She accepted the baby and all the life she brought to their lives.

From the first moment she met her as a cherubic two-year-old, Mother B understood the basic circumstances of Dorothy's beginning. In her own words about learning of the child's history:

> "Before taking the baby in, the history of the baby as given to me by my sister and Mr. Stuart was that her name was Zimmer; that her father was a lawyer, lived in Petersburg, Virginia; that her mother was a beautiful girl from a very prominent Virginia family; that she was born in wedlock but a few months too soon after the marriage; and that she had been kept by a Mrs. Watson since her birth. Dr. Lawrence said he could show the record of the child's birth and even offered to take Mr. Stuart to Petersburg to prove the parentage. I did not particularly care about it as I intended to raise the baby as my own."

Bertha did not have a plan, however, for the moment when Dorothy would learn the facts for herself. As any mother would, Bertha wanted to protect her child:

> "The revelations which have come to Dorothy have naturally made a profound impression on her, to the detriment of her peace of mind, especially in view of the facts which have been learned as to her real parents, their life, and social position, and their seeming abandonment of her, and for

her sake Mr. Hardy and I have deemed it proper to make the facts a matter of permanent record, solely out of my affection and love for her and for such preservation and use by her as she may desire and see fit to make. Otherwise, to us she remains our child as she has always been."

She encouraged Dorothy to seek answers. She wanted to remove the shroud of shame and secrecy that enveloped her daughter's existence.

The Hardys had always known about the baby's real parents, but at the time she took in baby Dorothy, Bertha's focus was on adapting to life with her new daughter. She loved the baby as her own and had no care for her backstory, impropriety or not. Getting her clothed, photographed, outfitted with dolls – these were her appropriate priorities. Baby Dorothy was the child she always wanted. Giving the baby the best life she could was her sole motivation.

In the back of Bertha's mind, she knew this day might come. She knew when and if it arrived, she would tell Dorothy the truth.

--
Secrets Buried in Petersburg

The Hardys' priest at the Catholic Church in Indian Head was also a close family friend who knew the Hardys well. Dorothy had always been so conscientious and dedicated student of music, Father Dillon noticed that she had not been herself that summer when practicing her organ before Mass. He wanted to see his bright young parishioner reconcile her troubles.

The Priest assured Mother B she was doing the right thing by seeking the truth. And he offered to help in any way he could.

Bertha seized the moment.

"Do you know a Priest in Petersburg?" Bertha asked.

"Yes, I do. Why?" the Priest probed.

"I wonder if you could arrange for Dorothy to stay in Petersburg so she can find what she needs?" Bertha pondered aloud.

He kindly obliged to find out for her. He telephoned the office of Petersburg's St. Joseph's Catholic Church. Within a couple of weeks, Dorothy was the house guest of a St. Joseph's parishioner, Miss Grace Bonjonia.

Miss Bonjonia was an older woman who knew Petersburg well and opened her home to this young woman searching for answers. With a home base, Dorothy could travel throughout Petersburg's streets, bouncing between the library, courthouse, and churches.

Dorothy's skills as a sleuth found purpose in her mission of digging for facts about her birth family.

She spent hours poring over pages stored between the courthouse walls. She found wills, agreements, and death records. She was agog at what she uncovered.

She camped out at the Petersburg Public Library, too. There she found an endless treasure trove of newspapers documenting the charmed lives of Sam and Polly and other Zimmers. Transatlantic cruises, weekends in Virginia Beach, society parties at 244 South Sycamore - details of her real family's life stood there in newsprint right before her eyes. They lived a perfect-appearing, vibrant life.

Curious about the true cause of death, Dorothy also paid a visit to the Virginia Office of Vital Statistics to see what time they opened the next morning. Miss Bonjonia had already confirmed what Dorsey Waters told her weeks earlier - that Dorothy's birth mother, Polly, had died three years ago.

When she walked up to the doors of the office building, she saw that they opened at 8am. She returned to Miss Bonjonia's home to retire for the day, intending to return to Vital Statistics when it opened first thing in the morning.

The fact that she was deceased was not enough to ease Dorothy's curious mind. She wanted to see Polly's death record for herself, which she thought might contain details of how – *and why* -- she died. So many questions rang through her head. Why would a beautiful woman of such prominence die so young when she seemingly "had it all?"

She was the first one at the door the next morning. Finally, she was about to find resolution to the questions burning in her mind.

Mary Blair Pryor Zimmer. Certificate of Death, #13255, issued by the Commonwealth of Virginia, Bureau of Vital Statistics.

Polly Zimmer's death certificate was signed and dated June 24, 1928, just two weeks after Dorothy's 19th birthday.

```
Full name: Mary Blair Pryor Zimmer.
Residence: 244 S. Sycamore St., Petersburg.
Length of residence where death occurred: 19
years. Female. White. Married.
Spouse: Samuel Watts Zimmer.
Age: 40 years, three months, 27 days.

"I hereby certify, that I attended deceased from
June 19 to June 24, 1928."

"And that death occurred, on date stated above,
at 8:30 AM"

"The cause of death was as follows: poisoning
self-administered, suicide intent"

Informant: Wm. L. Zimmer, Jr.
Signed, "C.G. Pleasants, Justice of Peace,
Acting Coroner."
```

What sadness in this discovery. What *sadness* Polly endured, that she would end her life while her son and daughter were so beautifully young at 15 and 17. Her daughter would turn 18 just one month later, and her mother would not be there to oversee celebrations.

The lovely, ever-attractive Polly, of American revolution and confederate royalty, suffered from such private misery. Misery she did not endure.

"What sadness," Dorothy thought, reading with her own eyes, the legal and recorded evidence for that upon which others had merely speculated.

Polly's life ended in tragedy. Polly did not accidentally "overdose." She did not die from alcoholism or pills. Dorothy's search – a search for any information about the woman who delivered her to life -- delivered death.

She died from poisoning, *self-administered with suicide intent*. The acting coroner, a justice of the peace in his regular job, noted "intent."

She lived for four days and died on the fifth morning after her self-poisoning. Her son William and her daughter Polly most certainly would have been at her side, unless Sam covered her death from them, just as he had hidden Dorothy's existence.

What Dorothy did know, is that her brother, William, a mere 15 years of age, and Polly, her mother's and grandmother's namesake of 17 years, lost their mother too young. She could see from society pages that her siblings remained in Petersburg with their father, who had been the city's mayor and civic leader.

Dorothy's siblings would be raised to adulthood by their Aunt Margaret Zimmer, affectionately called "Puggy." Puggy was their special aunt who never married, and their new matriarch for the remainder of their lives.

Polly and William surely found safety under Puggy's towering protection. William and Polly undoubtedly stayed attached to one another, and remained thick as thieves, not knowing they had an older sister who could have shared in their bond.

Dorothy continued forth with her research in Petersburg, poring through the newspaper stacks in the public library. She grazed past more pages from the late 1920's seeing her family members' names.

What she found reported in the *Petersburg Progress-Index* on Monday, June 25, 1928, stunned her again:

> "Mrs. Samuel W. Zimmer died at her home. 244 S. Sycamore Street at 8:30 o'clock Sunday morning. Funeral services will be held at the home tomorrow morning at 11 o'clock with internment in Blandford.
>
> Mrs. Zimmer is survived by her husband, Samuel Watts Zimmer, and two children, Miss Polly Zimmer and William Zimmer, and her mother, Mrs. Mary Walker, all of this city. She was before her marriage Miss Mary Blair Pryor Walker, daughter of Mrs. Mary Blair Pryor Walker, and the late Frank T. Walker, and grand-daughter of General Roger A. Pryor, noted New York lawyer."

Dorothy wasn't prepared to see her mother Polly's death reported in the paper. She was aware that meeting Polly alive would never happen, but an immense sadness came over her when the realization hit that all she would know of her mother was written in newsprint as her cause of death.

On one hand, she accepted Polly was dead and, on the other, she marveled at how her parents lived such public lives, yet managed to succeed in concealing her own existence.

Some part of her had hoped Polly was alive, somewhere, perhaps in secret, as she herself had been a secret.

Reading the words describing the hour of Polly's death made it real and sealed the fate that Dorothy would never share physical space with her mother. She saw how the newspaper article concealed the cause of death. Dorothy mourned Polly. She shed tears there in the library for the mother she would never know.

Dorothy could never know what role, if any, Polly played in her abandonment. Her death "with suicide intent" convinced Dorothy – perhaps mistakenly – that her life must have been deeply sad, even tortured, since losing two children.

As Dorothy obsessively scoured the library's collection of newspapers for the name Zimmer, she got quicker at deciphering the types of things to look for.

Social happenings featured Polly.

City Council reports featured Sam.

Ceremonies documented their joint attendance as "Mr. and Mrs. Sam Zimmer."

In scanning the newsprint with her finger, Dorothy's finger touching the black ink would be the closest she would get to her birth parents.

Dorothy's scanning was deliberate, efficient, and focused. She took copious notes. She wasn't sure exactly what she continued to look for, other than any and all additional data concerning the Zimmers.

She saw the very small announcement of Sam's remarriage to Alverda just months after Polly's death. Sam did not have an elaborate social event for his second marriage as he had done when he married Polly twenty years earlier. Dorothy studied the months between Polly's death and Sam's remarriage. Though no relationship expert, Dorothy's eyebrows raised high when she saw how quickly Sam remarried after Polly's tragic passing.

She gained proficiency at scanning the voluminous pages. The repetitiveness of her scanning shielded her from most of what her eyes were reading. But something new stopped her dead in her tracks.

OF MARY BLAIR DESTINY

The *Petersburg Progress-Index* had printed Sam's obituary, too, yet it was notably longer than his wife Polly's from three years earlier.

Former Mayor of Petersburg Dies in Norfolk

Samuel Zimmer Succumbs to Injuries Sustained when hit by Auto

Petersburg, Va., May 4, 1931

Funeral services for Samuel W. Zimmer, 47, Attorney, Banker, former Mayor, and one of Petersburg's most prominent citizens, who died in Norfolk this morning of injuries received when run down by an automobile in Norfolk Saturday night, will be held Wednesday afternoon at 5 o'clock at his home. Interment will be in Blandford Cemetery. The body was brought to Petersburg this afternoon from St. Vincent's Hospital, where Mr. Zimmer died this morning at 9:30 o'clock the result of a fractured skull, without regaining consciousness after having been struck.

Mr. & Mrs. Zimmer went to Virginia Beach Saturday afternoon to spend the weekend at the resort. They were returning to Norfolk about 9 o'clock Saturday night when Mr. Zimmer stopped his auto on the Virginia Beach Boulevard near the city limits, to get cigarettes in a store across the street. He was on his way back to his machine when struck by the automobile driven by J.C. Holland of Norfolk. He was hurled to the pavement rendered unconscious and suffered a fractured skull. Little hope for his recovery was held from the time he was taken to St. Vincent's. A number of specialists from Richmond, this city, and Norfolk were called in an effort to save his life.

Samuel Watts Zimmer

Says Accident "Unavoidable"
According to reports from Norfolk, Holland was charged with "assault with an automobile." He claimed the accident was unavoidable, saying that Mr. Zimmer had stepped directly in front of the machine which was headed toward Virginia Beach.

Mr. Zimmer was prominent in legal, financial, and social circles of Petersburg. For nearly 9 years, he had served as president of the Petersburg Savings and American Trust Company and the Petersburg Insurance Company. Prior to his election to these posts he served on the boards of directors for a number of years. At the time of his death, Mr. Zimmer, also was president to the Petersburg, Hopewell, and City Point Railway Company and Richmond-Ashland Railway Company.

Elected to City Council in 1921, Mr. Zimmer served for six years, during which time he also served as Mayor. He also served one term as Commonwealth's Attorney of Petersburg. During the World War he was stationed at San Antonio, Texas, with the rank of Major as judge advocate.

Native of Petersburg
A Native of Petersburg and the son of the later William L. Zimmer, one of Petersburg's leading tobacconists. Mr. Zimmer was educated at Episcopal High School and the University of Virginia, where he graduated in 1908. He took a prominent part in campus activities, at the University. He was a member of the Westmoreland Club, Richmond; Country Club of Petersburg and Petersburg Lodge of Elks. He was a communicant of Christ Episcopal Church and until about a year ago was treasurer of the Bishop Payne Divinity School here.

Mr. Zimmer is survived by his wife, Mrs. Alverta Edgerton Jones Zimmer, one daughter, Miss Polly Zimmer, one son William L. Zimmer III, one brother William L. Zimmer Jr., and three sisters, Miss Margaret Zimmer, Petersburg, Mrs. John Moyer, Richmond, and Mrs. Floyd Rogers, Asheville, N.C.

"Unavoidable," the driver of the car said of hitting Sam. Who in his right mind steps out onto a highway without first seeing the headlights coming in the distance? ...without first hearing the noisy unmuffled exhaust? ...without feeling the vibration of a speeding oncoming car? Cars in 1931 were certainly loud, with unmuffled exhaust pipes that would have been roaring at high speeds on a highway.

Was the impending reveal of Sam's old secret's finally too much for him? Did he purposefully step in front of that car on the highway outside Norfolk?

Sam's death certificate stated the official cause of death as "cerebral hemorrhage." The car struck him and hurled his head to the pavement. He never recovered despite being rushed to the hospital.

The coroner who examined Sam's body said, "There's something that always bothered me about Sam's death. He pulled over on the side of the road, his second wife was in the car. He pulled over, and got out the car. He walked right in front of a car that was coming toward him."

When Dorothy was investigating and looking for records of Sam's death, she sought out the coroner who discussed the case with her.

The coroner assessed, "If I had known that you were on Sam's trail, I wouldn't have ruled it was an accident."

He continued, "it just looked off and like a suicide from the beginning. The guy who was driving the car said he saw him get out the car and he just walked right in front of him." Whatever the case was, this was an accident that Sam's power and money could not allay for him.

The newspaper reported on the many people who mourned Sam's passing, the Mayor, the local leader. His first daughter, Dorothy, would learn of his existence and his death just weeks later. She also felt intense mourning, just the same. Mourning for his life, mourning for her life, but mostly mourning for the questions left unanswered.

Just as in his life, in his death she was left out of Sam's bio. But weeks after his official funeral, she would step upon the freshly placed soil at his grave side and wonder who had attended his funeral from her family that never was.

What Dorothy also did not know: Mother B visited Polly's grave just two months before on her own silent trek to Petersburg. Bertha sought to explore the "Zimmer" name on her own. When Dorothy innocuously asked for her birth certificate in March, Bertha knew that moment was just the beginning of what would become an avalanche of questions from Dorothy.

Bertha realized in March that the truth finally would be coming out. To prepare herself for that inevitability, she contacted Dr. Lawrence's office in D.C. She knew they had the original birth certificate.

Bertha also visited Petersburg. She asked questions so she could give Dorothy answers when the moment came. She connected the dots of the birth family quietly in advance of sharing anything with Dorothy.

Sam was still alive in May when Bertha visited Petersburg asking questions and bringing up the Zimmer name. Dorothy did not know about this visit until years later. Bertha wished to let Dorothy discover details as she wanted and could handle to know them. Perhaps, however, Sam did know that someone was bringing out the truth he had escaped two decades earlier.

Make this Affirmation today:
"I now affirm that I am resilient in the face of setbacks."

Sam's Apology

Oh, Dorothy, dear, how will you ever forgive me?
Please do hold me harmless, as you do mother Polly.

When you discover the fullness of what had to be done,
I hope you see tranquility again in each day's setting sun.

Let the golds and reds of June's summer's evening
Not be a searing reminder of your parents' leaving.

Try being lost in mother nature's grand beauty,
Please don't curse my name and your mother's lost purity.

Each birthday you celebrate in every future year's June –
I hope you feel 'happy birthday' not your birth's dire misfortune.

What will you do when your skills as a sleuth
Show the lengths I went to hide you, your truth?

And that skill you have for snooping, just know from where it came.
From me! Yes, indeed, you have my brilliant mind, just not my regal name.

I do hope you learn nothing, but in case one day you do,
Just know it was never meant to be, us keeping you.

The crush of June is your eternal tax due for this bounty called life,
And your amnesty is begged on my behalf and that of my wife.

I do know the burden you bear – true, it's yours borne alone.
Yet I hope forgiveness soothes your soul, my beautiful clone.

My death prevents our reunion, so you may ask with this why I bother,
Because gaining forgiveness for my faults is my last quest –
Love, Your Father.

February, 1937, Marriage of Dorothy Stuart Hardy to A.M. Bryan

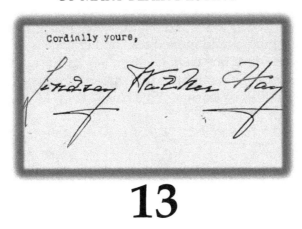

13

--
Great Souls Are Quiet – 1932.

> *But why should I ask my readers to listen while I press, "like Philomel, my heart against a thorn!" We can change nothing in our lives. We must bear the lot ordained for us! We need not ask others to suffer with us! Grosse seelen dulden still*
> Sara Rice Pryor, 1910

Her life had been going along rather ordinarily. She was in motion. She had a good young man as her boyfriend. Despite the Depression that had set in for so many Americans, she was still doing pretty well with her civil service job.

Learning the truth about her birth, her parents, and their life had come out nowhere as total surprise and brought with it unknowable uncertainties. Mother B loved her no less for wanting to know more about her birth family. In fact, she fully supported Dorothy in pursuing whatever truths she needed. Bertha just wanted Dorothy to find peace and settle her soul. Dorothy launched forward in searching for anything, everything she could find in a quest to know.

When Dorothy returned from her Petersburg sojourn, she could not comprehend all that she had learned. She soon resigned from her job at the Census bureau and moved back to her childhood home in Indian Head to readjust. She went to church every Sunday and began giving piano lessons again but otherwise had not returned to her normal buoyant self since learning "the news" from Mother B.

Dark words from Polly's 1928 death certificate rang in Dorothy's head each day.

"Poisoning self-administered, suicide intent."

These dark words clashed with her image of the perfect-appearing, charmed life that was depicted in pages upon pages of Petersburg society news. What was the explanation for the disparity between Polly's life and her death? Dorothy could not decipher the truth for herself, nor could she release herself from the urge to know more.

Dorothy continued to write letters to her new-found cousin Dorsey, sharing details of her research in every installment. Dorsey, too, was greatly surprised to learn that Polly had intentionally killed herself. Family members had only told him that she died of an "accidental overdose" during a terrible migraine episode. Dorsey always presumed Polly was the one who had it the best of the three Walker sisters. He, presumably like many others, was surprised by the tragic way her life ended, and Dorothy's research was raising questions even he had not considered. He cared deeply for and accepted Dorothy. He wanted to help her, too.

Dorsey talked about an aunt, Lindsay Walker Hay, to Dorothy on more than one occasion, piquing her interest. Instantly, she intended to meet this aunt who was the only remaining living sister of her birth mother.

Dorothy thought surely "Aunt Lindsay" would share an eagerness to meet and connect with her long-lost niece. She pinned big wishes on meeting Lindsay, hoping for a warm reunion and answers. Hoping Lindsay would be willing to connect her to her surviving siblings, William and Polly, and to other extended family, Dorothy looked forward to meeting Lindsay. This was as close to meeting her actual mother as she would ever get, she reasoned.

As it turned out, Aunt Lindsay was aghast and resistant at the mere thought of meeting Dorothy. This episode was not a skeleton Lindsay wished to pull out of the family's closet of secrets. She knew the gravity of what it meant for Dorothy's existence to be revealed, much less details about how her abandonment truly occurred.

Lindsay worried that unearthing this secret would only lead to bad things: Sullied reputations; Tarnished legacies; Disgrace; Ugly truths; Unattractiveness. Confusion. With Sam and Polly both deceased, it was all left well enough in the past, with no need to dredge up the unfortunate event. She most definitely would not be helping anyone know more.

Lindsay knew exactly what she felt toward Dorothy: Hostility. She did not hold feelings of elation in finding a long-lost niece, as Dorothy had so hoped. Upon their first meeting, Lindsay graciously informed her new-found niece that she was to go away and keep quiet for good. She threatened to sue Dorothy if any part of her story or existence was ever revealed.

"Do you understand how many lives you would ruin?" Lindsay admonished unknowing Dorothy. Lindsay was thinking of her niece and nephew, Polly and William, and how the discovery of their parents' disgrace would only further complicate their lives. They were already survivors of both their mother and father's untimely tragic deaths. For Lindsay, it was simply unfathomable that Polly and William might actually welcome an older sister in their fold, especially now. In any case, it was too big of a risk.

This was not about truth versus lies. This was not about mystery. Lindsay knew good and well that Dorothy was telling the truth. She knew about the 1909 hidden pregnancy. She knew that the orphaned baby was left behind. The truth was not her concern. The truth was ugly, and she knew that.

Yet, there was no denying truth – the secret baby was staring back at Lindsay, now as an adult woman. Lindsay knew exactly what she was looking at when she saw that same face in Dorothy as she had seen in Sam. Dorothy was his spitting image. None of it mattered. Reality was staring her in the face.

Perhaps Lindsay projected her culpability in preserving the lies as anger onto Dorothy. After all, Lindsay was Polly and Sam's decades-long accomplice in hiding of the secret pregnancy and baby. Perhaps her anger was a primordial "NOOOO!" derived deep within her. She could withstand no more upending life events.

To Dorothy's disappointment, Lindsay threatened her with lawsuits one day, yet next was calm and solicitous, sending gifts to Dorothy and her babies. Lindsay would prove to be an elusive, cool holder of secrets. She wrote nice letters, but at first would not sign them with her real name, for fear of being linked to an inglorious remnant of her dead sister's life.

Dorothy saw Lindsay with clear eyes. When she first opened communications, Lindsay sent Dorothy letters without a name, return address or any signature. When returning with her own letters, Dorothy responded in kind with notes unsigned. This was not in deference to or flattering imitation of Lindsay. No – it was to square her on her incivility. Her small-town upbringing was intolerant of such chicanery.

Though Dorothy originally hoped Lindsay would give answers and be a link to lost family, she was thoroughly unwilling to offer help in any way. In fact, if anything, Lindsay actively undermined Dorothy's quest. When first learning of Dorothy's existence and desire to connect with Zimmers, Lindsay surreptitiously alerted the surviving Zimmers. At first strike, she clouded their perception of Dorothy and her intent. Lindsay effectively prevented any contact Dorothy attempted and was a conduit for continued rejection, not reunion. She was a dead-end, not a pathway.

Sadly, Lindsay more than anyone knew Dorothy's story was true, yet she never revealed to the Zimmers the full story. Of course, she knew fully about Polly's hidden pregnancy in D.C. in spring of 1909. She fed the Zimmers information about Dorothy, and misled Dorothy, leading her to believe that she wanted a genuine relationship.

The worst part of Lindsay's position was that she was duplicitous with Dorothy about her intent. She was of two mouths: She gave Dorothy hope by maintaining contact with her, yet she nourished fear in the Zimmers by telling them that Dorothy was only after money. Lindsay relished having a purpose with the Zimmers, even if she was a roadblock to reunion.

Instead of family reunion, she found adversaries. What Dorothy hoped would be a reunion turned into a battle of wits, with her stubbornly determined to prove that she was Sam and Polly's child. Mother B supported her still, and helped her follow through with proving herself. This was not an approach to life with which Dorothy was familiar. Protecting legacies, maintaining appearances at the expense of blood relatives was foreign. Dorothy simply wanted connection and to know something – anything – about her parents and siblings.

Lindsay wrote to Dorothy inviting her to join her for seasonal lunches. She invited her to her home, yet forbid her from meeting its occupants. Polly Walker, by then an elderly grandmother, also lived there with Lindsay, yet remained shut away in a private room behind a closed door whenever Dorothy visited. Dorothy was expressly forbidden from entering that room, and she complied. Lindsay never introduced Dorothy to the woman that was her natural grandmother, merely feet away.

Lindsay and Dorothy continued to write and had cordial meetings in person for a few years. As long as Dorothy avoided all sensitive subjects, such as the name Zimmer, or any topic having to do with family of any kind, everything was pleasant.

The glib cordiality eventually fizzled between Dorothy and Lindsay. Instead of closing a broken loop, Lindsay would be the linchpin keeping the secret closed off forever and never revealed.

Despite Lindsay's rejection, Dorsey ended up facilitating Dorothy's quest. He helped her learn their family history, the origin of the Mary Blair name, and he connected impossible dots.

Dorsey was both merciful and genuine. He confirmed she was not crazy. Dorothy and Dorsey remained close friends. He became her future husband's hunting buddy and surrogate uncle to her children – all seven of them.

Dorothy collected herself and moved on, busily creating her own family. She remained quiet.

September 11, 1939

My dear Dorothy:

        Do you think it would be possible for you to take lunch with me some time in the near future, on a Saturday? You could meet me at the same entrance to the Department of Justice Building, 10th Street and Pennsylvania Avenue, N.W., at about a quarter past one, if that will suit you.

        Much as I would like to see the baby I am not going to ask you to bring her, for I know how much trouble it entails, and I do not think it is any too good for the child. However, if you have a picture of her, or a snapshot, I would love to see it. I saw the one taken by Edmondson, but I have seen nothing of her since.

        Let me hear from you when you can,

                      Affectionately yours,

                      Lindsay Walker Hay

14

The Soil Turned in Blandford Cemetery

Sam's body is buried adjacent to the mother of his children, Polly, and their infant son, Samuel, Jr. The Zimmers' plot at the Blandford Cemetery on the edge of Petersburg rests near a hill's crest, in the shadows of a towering Confederate monument. Blandford's rich Virginia soils hold the flesh and bones of American Revolutionaries, thousands of Confederate soldiers, and the tears of their mourners. And the celebrants of emancipation.

As Dorothy sat at the foot of Polly's grave for the first time, her mother who died in the Petersburg summer heat of 1928, she wondered who else's feet stood on this same soil over the solemn comings and goings of years.

Dorothy's very own feet were standing upon this soil. Her tears dropped on its soil. When Dorothy first visited Blandford Cemetery in 1931, she had just learned of Polly's existence, and, then in a wallop, of her death. As her eyes studied the tall marble monuments and the rolling hills of Blandford, she noticed the loose soil around Sam's grave. It was freshly displaced from his recent burial. Just weeks before, had her siblings stood in this very spot, looking at the same soil, mourning the loss of not only their father, but their mother buried adjacent to him?

No doubt, when Polly was buried in 1928 her other two children wept on this soil.

Sam must have also stood there upon the same soil in 1928 – did he think he administered his own emotional poison, a poison of attractive deception for their 19 years of matrimony? Did Sam weep on this soil where his secret daughter sat? Or did he breathe in relief that his secrets were now buried six feet under with Polly?

Did Polly's mother, Polly Pryor Walker, weep on this soil? Did she weep at this sad ending to her namesake-daughter's life when she died so young? Did she know of her daughter's secret baby?

Did Roger and Sara Pryor weep on this soil where Dorothy was now weeping? Did they take the train from New York to Petersburg to bury their beautiful young granddaughter Polly? Did Sara chronicle her grandchildren's lives the way she chronicled the confederacy? Surely, Sara's appetite for history included the 'present' of her children and grandchildren. Surely, she knew her grandchildren's activities back in Petersburg. Are her footprints on this soil beside Dorothy's?

Surely, mother Polly Pryor Walker stood on this soft soil, too, watching and weeping as her daughter's body was laid to rest too young. Giving comfort to her grandchildren William and Young Polly, she may have wondered as any mother if her son-in-law was hiding malfeasances. Did she look at him differently? Did she hold him responsible?

In the back of Polly Sr.'s mind, did she know her daughter tolerated Sam's ways – the philandering ways an entitled, ambitious man of his day enjoyed, even if she did not have evidence? Did it startle her, in 1928, that she'd lost two of her three daughters to suicide? Did she openly wonder why, or did she keep her wonderings to herself, in private quarters of her mind, if at all?

Did she ask herself why they sacrificed their own lives – and their children's lives – to fit into the lives of their men and social position? Did she question whether she had done enough to strengthen them? Did she question if her own push for absolute perfection damaged her daughters' psyches?

Did she wonder why money and position did not appease her two daughters' misery? Surely, she had wanted for them to regain the stature that her parents had lost after the Civil War, the calamity that bankrupted their attractive, deeply-respected, fine Virginia family.

Of course, Polly Sr. knew that her daughters did very well in marrying, yet at what cost? Did she look at their graves and see that their marriages cost them their very lives?

Polly Sr. likely knew in the back of her mind that her daughter Polly's suicide may never have happened if she had never crossed paths with the dashing young Sam, on the lush lawns of UVA. Frances was always the less stable daughter, and she always saw Polly as the best hope among her children. Frances' suicide was horrific, but far less surprising.

Polly Sr.'s best hopes for Polly Walker Zimmer lived no longer. Polly Sr. herself would die in the spare bedroom in her divorced, last-remaining daughter's apartment in D.C. She died with a legacy intact. Yet she died alone and not knowing her lost granddaughter, perhaps not even caring to know her. A legacy was intact, indeed.

Did William III, Sam's only son, weep for his mother and father on this Blanchard Cemetery soil? Did he weep here for his mother's private sorrow? Did he revere his father for his ambition, achievements, and status? Or did William III ever see through Sam's veneer, knowing his father's public gentility was duplicitous?

Dorothy did not weep for Sam. She wondered though, who did weep for Sam on this soil? Who loved this man who abandoned her, his flesh and blood?

Did his new wife of less than a year weep for Sam? Alverta reserved her spot next to his grave for her death in 1945. Strange that their marriage occurred so quickly following Polly's tragic death just months before. Perhaps their relationship was in progress; Perhaps she loved him, as his children adored him.

Inches from Polly's grave, perhaps brother William's own children and grandchildren wept on the same soil for him? The inches belittle the vastness of mystery. This grandmother Polly is one they would only know in stories, but never meet.

Who stood where? Did William's daughter come bringing her adult children with her from Florida? Did they say to themselves, "William is with his mother now?" Did they whisper to him as he died, *'Polly is waiting for you, go be with Polly.'* Did William's nieces in Louisville come for his funeral?

The soil is soft in Blanchard cemetery, and the air is crisp and sweet. Many souls have blown through here while the silence of their stories is forever kept.

In her first visit to Blandford in 1931, Dorothy would not know when she sat at her dead parents' graves, that all of her own future brood would also later visit their graves. She did not know her own children would become productive, regular people with ordinary, good things and wholesome success in their lives. Dorothy's future family – yet to be started – would have their share of challenges, but nothing that would ever cause any one of them to tragically succumb as Sam and Polly did.

Dorothy must have thought about all of this when she visited Petersburg without fail every year. She drove by 244 S. Sycamore, stopping her car on the roadside, only able to see it from the curb each time. As she drove a few miles away to the cemetery, what thoughts circled in her mind? How many times did she drive by each visit? What emotion pulsed through her as she steered her throughout the town?

ERIN L. RICHMAN

She walked up to the edge of her mother Polly's grave, observing:

"POLLY WALKER ZIMMER,
1888 - 1928,
HER INFANT SON
SAM'L W. ZIMMER, JR.
1916."

As she drove away from the cemetery of her mother and father, was she gripped by anger at never knowing them? Or perhaps sorrow? Or gratitude? Did she speak to her mother's grave as she stood over it? How many times did she drive by South Sycamore?

What did Dorothy feel thirty years later in 1962, when she herself was a mother to seven and grandmother and realized she was now older than her own Mother had been when she died? There's nothing to do in a cemetery except look at dates and think about the lives behind the names of the dead. One cannot escape from mortality and fleetingness of time when staring upon the dates of the dead.

As an old woman in the latter years of her life, how did she feel when she visited with her very own daughter, Mary Blair, and also with her namesake granddaughter, Mary Blair? How many other times did she visit that are unknown? Dorothy visited her blood family's plot in Blandford always as an outsider, looking upon the life and deaths of a family she felt she was denied.

Finally, in 1986, Dorothy visited Petersburg for one of the last times, visiting the beautiful mansion at 244 South Sycamore. The home had become the offices of the Episcopal Diocese and was no longer a private residence. She and Mary Blair parked their car and entered through the immense iron gates for the very first time.

As Dorothy walked up the sidewalk toward the front landing, she took each step carefully. She stopped. The moment was not lost on her.

This was the place – the very same home – where her mother and father hosted hundreds of guests for *'the social event of the season'* following their surprise wedding in Washington. This was the place – the very same home – where they returned after abandoning her in Washington. This was where they raised their *claimed* children.

These were the steps they walked as they carried on with their lives. These are the boxwoods her siblings played hide-and-seek in during the childhoods she did not share with them.

This was also where Polly poisoned herself and died.

Dorothy paused, took a deep breath. She reflected, knowing she would finally see its interior. She took it all in. The furniture inside was the Zimmer family's that had been gifted to the Diocese with the house.

She sat in the now-antique wood chairs. She sat at the head of the dining room table. She sat in the entry way.

As she left its heavy wooden front door, she stopped once more. There, at the homestead of the family that abandoned her 76 years before, she stood proudly, impeccably, and fierce. Now, she finally knew how it felt to hold the iron railings and to stand perched on the porch overlooking the impeccable gardens.

Now that she was in it, she claimed it – even if it would never claim her.

It is no wonder that younger sister Polly would marry and leave Virginia for the rest of her life, moving to Louisville and escaping the ghosts of her mother and father in Petersburg. Her children would never know their grandparents. Yet she created them a life anew far away in Kentucky, always with fond remembrances of old Virginia. In the end, sister Polly did the same thing that older sister Dorothy had done, only by choice. They had in common their parents, their birth names, as well as their escape of their dark legacy. They recreated their lives in stark contrast to the dark secrets buried in Petersburg and instead chose to focus on the happier parts of their legacies.

And there it was. Embedded in the 1950's newspaper image was the announcement that sister Polly and her husband Archibald would be visiting Petersburg, Virginia, on their way to France. They would be visiting their two daughters, Polly and Lee, as well as their niece, all of whom were spending the summer studying abroad *en France*.

Dorothy's brother, William, had just one daughter. Her comings and goings with her Zimmer cousins were noteworthy enough to get mention in the Petersburg newspaper's social pages. It was a different era, to be sure, but not everyone was worthy of mention in the paper. Their departures to France and return to Petersburg were announced in the news pages, as if it were assumed that someone out there *should* and would want to know.

One can only imagine how idyllic the lives of these young women were, the granddaughters of Sam and Polly, the niece and nephew of Dorothy and cousins to her children. They were young women of affluence who were seeing and experiencing the world. A world still friendly to Americans and a world full of optimism in the post-War booming economy of the 50's.

Dorothy pictured them with perfectly coifed American hair, trim skirts and blouses, with their scarves whipping in the Paris wind as they scurried out of museums onto the Champs Elysees. Were they confident, bubbling young American women exploring the world? Were they debutantes traveling in a post-War France, a country thankful for the superpower of the United States and welcoming the sounds of Elvis into their radio airwaves?

Indeed, they were *the* young *elite* Americans, and the world was literally at their fingertips. Travel empowers the young to feel they can do anything, be anything, and expect to have everything. Travel helps us all dream of the world beyond and grow new branches.

It is a stark divergence to imagine the Zimmer grandchildren spending summers traversing the French countryside, while imagining summers of their seven secret cousins in Indian Head, Maryland. Imagining the rowdy Catholic girls stealing smokes behind the gym with their friends is rather amusing. The secret seven were probably doing what other teens in the 1950's did – listening and dancing to Elvis and feeling a good bit naughty. They were the young, *randy* Americans. Maybe they had that in common with their cousins.

In an alternate universe, William Zimmer was simply Dorothy's baby brother. Had she known him, she would have been in his world, the world of blue bloods and the aristocrats-to-be of Virginia – hell, of the U.S. for that matter. Virginia is where Presidents are born, after all.

Their weddings were announced in the *New York Times* and other papers. Dorothy ensured her events were announced in the papers, too.

Dorothy would have attended all of her brother William's football games at UVA out in the open in this alternate universe. She would have been proud of him when he lost to future-Supreme-Court-justice Lewis F. Powell for a delegate position to the American Bar Association. She would have given him big-sisterly advice and a pat on the back when his company, A.H. Robins Corporation, ran into a major legal mess with the Dalkon Shield lawsuits.

Dorothy, the big sister, would have been there for all of that. They corresponded a few times, and he knew of her. Love was never shared.

Instead, secret-sister grew up in a humble, middle-class life in a small town in southern Maryland. She sought and got her job in federal civil service. She went to church faithfully. She raised a tribe of her own.

Of course, they are probably perfectly nice, decent people as they live and weave amongst their neighbors. They seem so unreal. Theirs is an alternate universe, and perhaps that makes them more *not* part of *Dorothy's* family.

Or, perhaps, hers is not part of theirs. Is Dorothy's family too average? For sure, her tribe is a good-looking, law-abiding bunch, but they do have warts, as everyone does.

Perhaps their greatest fear is that they are somehow the outcasts, *the rejected. The bastards.*

They *were* the rejected. Their beloved Mother was discarded by people who were "too good" to keep her, which really meant they were too snooty. The best defense to rejection is to reject first. They believed they were the illegitimate branch, conceived out of wedlock; Abandoned; Surrendered; Nonexistent.

Yet, they did exist.

They were never to be known, never to be acknowledged, and never to become part of the Zimmer-Walker-Pryor legacy. As such, they created their own.

The deepest irony is that "they" – the children and grandchildren of Mary Blair Zimmer, aka Dorothy Stuart Hardy Bryan, probably never would have existed at all had "they" been acknowledged in the first place.

Remaining unacknowledged determined their branch's very existence. In fact, remaining unacknowledged *saved* their existence.

Had Dorothy been kept at birth, not abandoned, her children surely would not exist at all. Her branch of the Mary Blair family tree had to be separate in order to propagate and sprout the precise limbs that it did, thus beginning a whole new branch of the tree.

She would have never married the young man from Indian Head, Maryland, nor bore his seven children, at the precise times she did. They would have never given birth to the resulting 25 grandchildren, and 40+ great-grandchildren. Not only did she exist, she blossomed!

In the scheme of this family tree, Dorothy's abandonment was a *necessary* step. For her existence to have become a point on the large map of humanity, Sam preventing the doctor from showing the baby to Polly was a *necessary* step. Sam and Polly leaving the baby behind in shame was *necessary*.

Sam and Polly both dying young was *necessary* for her to become the good Catholic girl who made so many babies. Had they been alive when she discovered her true birth story, she most likely would have met them in person. Meeting them may have changed the path of her fact-finding in Petersburg from an independent sojourn to a homecoming, possibly changing her young life's path entirely.

For any glorious, splendid branch of this family tree to exist, the tragedy of its splitting was *necessary*. If the occasion of baby Dorothy's birth and subsequent abandonment had not unfolded as it did, the rest of the tree would not have grown exactly as it did. Perhaps what began as a scandal turned into a gift.

> "Do you realize how many events, choices, that had to occur since the birth of the universe leading up to the making of you? Just exactly the way you are."
>
> - From *A Wrinkle in Time*, Mrs. Which to Meg, written by Madeleine L'Engle

Dorothy Hardy Bryan, at 244 S. Sycamore St., Petersburg VA, in May, 1986. She stood on the former Zimmer family home, where Sam and Polly returned following her birth in Washington D.C. At age 76, this was the first and only time she would enter the property, as the stately home housed church offices at that time and was open to the public.

OF MARY BLAIR DESTINY

15

--
The Mother Line

We are all connected to our mothers. Whether we ever meet them or not, we are deeply connected to our mothers. We were formed within their wombs – literally one with them – as we came into being alive on this Earth. Whether we like it or not, there is a lifelong physical connection to our mother. The belly button on our abdomens is a reminder of the portal that once physically connected our cells and blood to theirs.

At one time we needed every single one of their breaths just as much as they needed it. We survived on their blood and oxygen; we needed them to live for us to live. Every single part of our body formed within and as part of hers. She was a vessel for our becoming and our being.

These are inescapable truths. Though our DNA is the product of both the mother and father's contributions, it is only the mother's body that nourishes our development and our emergence into living, into breathing – into *life*. It is the mother's body that not only carries us across the finish line, but also gives us legs, literally and figuratively.

Becoming one's own person – gaining autonomy – means that one day we actually choose (or not) to share physical space with our mothers. Yet, for those 9 months when we transitioned from a mere single cell to a fully-formed small human, we had no choice. We were sharing physical space with mother.

Everywhere she was, we were. Everything she heard, we heard. Every ray of light that hit her, hit us. We tasted her curries; our distaste for onions is probably actually her distaste that formed our own while we occupied her body.

Our connection to mother can be the source of our greatest comfort when we need love and a safe harbor from the crazy seas of this world. Our connection to mother can also be a source of anxiety, despair, and grief, depending on how she delivers her love and attachment to us, assuming she delivers them at all. Whether comfort or anxiety, love or despair, we are connected to her.

Yet, it is also motherhood's twisted torment that one day we, our mothers' children, grow up to be able to choose *not* to share physical space with our mother. Most humans do choose this. No doubt, despite their best gradual efforts to protect themselves from the pain caused by detaching from the most sublime attachment, our mothers are connected to us, too. For each one of us, our mothers spent nine long months giving her body over to us, whether she liked it or not.

She probably liked the tacit permission she had to eat whatever she wanted and indulge in an extra milkshake here and there. She probably marveled at the first time she felt us move in her lower abdomen. She grew so used to feeling us move within her body that she forgot what it felt like *not* to have a being moving within her. This is truly one of the most amazing sensations this life offers.

She probably liked that sensation of the baby's movement, even if it reminded her of the scary reality that she was soon bringing another life onto the planet. "How will I know what to do?" rang in her head every time she imagined taking care of her baby and all the things a mother must learn to do. Her hormones give her a head start to loving us.

In all likelihood, if she was nauseous, she did not love that part of her pregnancy. She probably didn't like the constipation, nor the constant pressure on her bladder that kept her keenly aware of all nearby restrooms.

Yet, whether she liked the physical particulars of pregnancy or not, every single day of pregnancy she was given a physical reminder of our existence in her body, of the imminence of our being in the world. With every uncomfortable toss and turn in the dead of the night – because her belly was too big to allow any achievable comfort horizontally – she was reminded that our body was inside hers and our presence was nearing.

When your mother carried you in her womb, she also carried your pint-sized organs. If you were a female, she carried your fully-formed, tiny-sized womb and ovaries also. For females, your mother, then, carried not only you, but she also carried and was connected to all of the eggs of your potential future children. A woman's lifetime supply of eggs in her ovaries were in her body just two months after she was conceived in mother's womb. All grandmothers carried not only their daughters in their womb, but all of the eggs that daughter would one day birth as her babies.

Siblings begin their physical journey together amongst thousands of eggs while inside their mother's fetal body – all while their mother is still forming inside their grandmother.

Every single human, then, is literally and physically connected to his or her maternal grandmother. When Granny was pregnant with your mother, she was carrying around the eggs in your mother's body that would one day make you. Every one of us, then, was once an egg forming in our grandmother's abdomen. And, thought of another way, every mother began her path to motherhood in the womb of her own mother, where the eggs of her future children would be formed.

Expectations for our future lives are usually handed to us by our mothers. For a few, the expectation is to marry well and preserve propriety. For most, it is to be happy and work hard. For an unfortunate few, their mothers do not care at all.

16

--
of Mary Blair Destiny

Mary Blair "Polly" Pryor Walker Zimmer entered motherhood when she birthed her children. By official record, she birthed three children in Petersburg, Virginia. Her lone 'official' daughter was Mary Blair "Polly" Zimmer born in 1910, and her only son was William III born in 1912. Among her three 'official' children was another son, Samuel, Jr., forever an infant when he died just two short days after his birth in 1916.

In secret, however, she actually birthed and named four children, including not one, but *two* daughters. Both were named Mary Blair.

In truth, her two Mary Blairs were born just thirteen months and 100 miles apart. They forever remained complete strangers to each other, even if the two Mary Blairs shared 100% of their parentage. These two daughters of Polly Pryor Walker Zimmer would forever be split branches of the same family tree.

Polly's first Mary Blair (III) was born in Washington D.C. on a Wednesday summer evening. The baby would be born in secret to her young mother who would never know her because the baby girl was whisked away from her mother immediately after she was born, in keeping with the father's unusual demands.

This baby, Mary Blair, would never be seen again by her mother, not even once. How could Polly, a first-time mother, endure a loss such as this? How could her husband prevent her from seeing it?

Exactly one year later, grieving the loss of her first baby daughter, Polly gave birth to her second daughter, and also named her Mary Blair, just as she had the secret baby. She then raised and knew this second baby daughter as most mothers normally know their babies. The daughters' names were identical, yes, but the circumstances of their lives were not. Had the first baby never existed, perhaps the second would not have either.

Both sisters lived as complete strangers.

The two Mary Blairs would grow in life as if they were parts of the same tree profoundly divided at its trunk, yet joined in its singular roots. Later, they would each create even more Mary Blairs, a fact which one imagines would have pleased Sara Pryor.

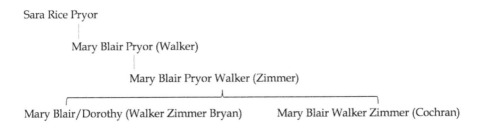

In fact, Sara's matrilineal naming precedent would be the only truly shared experiences of the two sister-Mary Blairs and their future daughters.

What each Mary Blair never knew is that another complete branch of Mary Blairs existed in a parallel world. The two branches were separate, but still in the name of the mother – matriarchal and matrilineal. The two separate lines of Mary Blairs were named for the same original Mary Blair, yet unaware of one another because the first had been born from of an old - yet familiar – stigma in Victorian-era America.

Her existence was a secret, and her birth would have caused a scandal. Her life began in lies, secrets, and denial.

Yet, for all her name's uniqueness, the first Mary Blair was born in circumstances that were neither regal, empowered, nor entirely unique. She entered the world and life began in a dirty rented boarding room in Washington, D.C.

Nonetheless, in these split sisters' lives, they would create a lot more Mary Blairs carrying Sara's naming precedent forward for generations.

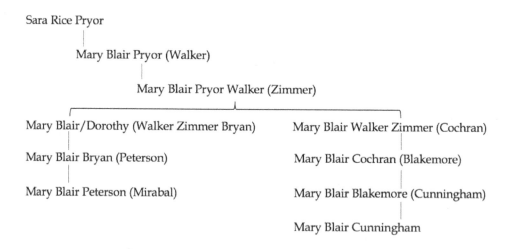

In the second branch of Mary Blairs, the second sister, Mary Blair Walker Zimmer (II), had a daughter, grand-daughter, and great-grand-daughter with her namesake. Four Mary Blair's grew from this branch in less than one century.

The first branch – a "secret" tribe of Mary Blairs – started with first-born sister named Mary Blair, who later became known as Dorothy Stuart Hardy Bryan after foster parents changed her name upon taking her into their home. Dorothy spawned her own very dense arbor of children and grandchildren.

Dorothy's first daughter, Elizabeth did not receive the name Mary Blair, as was practice in the Mary Blair naming ritual. When a second daughter was born, Dorothy hesitated. She did not name her for two full weeks – presumably because she was undecided. She must have been pondering whether to be so bold as claim her birth name, Mary Blair, for her own child, despite being outcast from the original line.

Boldly, if not altogether audacious, she named her second-born daughter Mary Blair. This daughter would grow up and name her own first-born daughter Mary Blair as well. Mary Blair Bryan Peterson and Mary Blair Peterson Mirabal made up the secret tribe of Mary Blairs. This line of women were full blood relatives to the first line.

The two branches of Mary Blairs diverged at the young, beautiful "Polly," Mary Blair Pryor Walker. Polly was born in a reeling reconstructing Virginia. It was a state rebuilding every aspect of itself after losing the bloody and destructive Civil War. She was, as perhaps none other could be, a daughter of the confederacy and the hope of her family's future.

When the family tree branch split, the two families were concealed from each other by a web of lies layered with deception and shame. Yet and still, by the year 1990, seven individual Mary Blairs would be living in two separate worlds.

The world of Dorothy, the first daughter, was one of the common working-class American. Attractiveness was a quality of one's appearance, not an absolute standard of perfection to maintain in all aspects of life. Working class parents aspired to provide upward mobility for their children, not maintain a stature achieved by grandfathers. Hers was a world scripted by work, family, and faith. And it was a world of moving forward, not preserving the past.

The world of the second daughter was one of refinement, perfect appearances, privilege, tradition, and secrets. Secrets concealed everything less than attractive out of view at any cost. This world was for the elite few, whose job it was to conserve and preserve the status quo.

They shared much in common, but would forever remain strangers.

17

Revealing Buried Scars

My mother, Trish, never wanted to be ashamed of us, her three daughters. Avoiding shame seemed like a fixation. I had a heightened awareness of shame, yet I never understood from where our family's fixation originated.

My mother had three daughters and raised us on her own after her marriage to my father ended. She taught us to be independent and self-sufficient. We mowed our own grass, we changed the oil in our cars, and we earned our own money. It was no secret she did not want us relying on any one else for support.

Being ashamed was one of the worst things we could cause her to feel. Thankfully, I felt how proud she was of us, but I certainly worked hard to avoid bringing her any shame. Shame was to be avoided. Like every daughter who wants her parent's approval, I wanted my mother's approval, too. But I mostly wanted to prevent feeling her glare of shame.

Fear of shame and embarrassment were infused in the air we breathed in our home. We may have been working class, but we had meters for judgment and shame built in us from birth. She expected us to comport ourselves with dignity and virtue.

I always assumed this was because we were Catholic, but I now know this infusion of shame was as much about our Granny's psychological burden as it was about our Catholicism, if not more the former.

Phrases I commonly heard from my mother included the energy of shame.

"Close your legs when you're sitting like that!"

"Do NOT make me have to come up to that school and hear about you getting in trouble."

"Do you want everyone to see you looking like that?"

"Girls don't do pushups like that."

"You get THAT from your father."

"That" in the last line refers to confidence and self-assuredness. Being comfortable in one's own skin – being confident – was somehow a character flaw that came from the cheater-womanizer type of person my father was. She did not really mean that she was not happy with who I was. Her criticisms of my confidence were more about her relationship with my father than about me. What I did not know as a child is how closely my mother associated my father's self-assuredness with her own strife and pain. With the advantage of adulthood, I can empathize with my mother's recoil at the cocky self-assuredness of others, even me, her youngest daughter.

"Mom, tell me about the night I was born," I asked one time when I was about 12, hopeful and curious about my entry to the world. I assumed I had a crowd of family awaiting my arrival at the hospital.

We were sitting in a restaurant booth, eating dinner, just the two of us alone, as my older sisters were at the age when they were frequently away from home with their teenage friends.

"Who was at the hospital? What time was I born?" I eagerly peppered her for details.

"You were born in the middle of the night," she told me, soberly.

"Who was in the room with you?" I quickly asked again, pressing for more, and missing her signal that this was not as exciting of a conversation for her as I thought it would be. I expected my mother would be excited to talk about the occasion of my birth.

"I don't remember," she said, letting me know in her quick tone that she wasn't trying that hard to remember.

"What do you mean, you 'don't remember'?" I scoffed.

"That was a long time ago," she said, trying to pretend having a bad memory.

"Mooooom, you have to remember something! Who was there?" I pressed. I was not settling for her evasiveness around these basic facts.

Sensing that her self-assured, fast-talking daughter was not going to let this go, she let a little out.

"Your Aunt Edie and her husband were there," she said, hoping to placate me.

"And who else?" I said, encouraging her to let the long list of people to begin flowing out of her mouth, expecting an avalanche of family members' names.

"I don't remember," she said in a huff, which was actually code for shutting down this line of questioning.

"Mom. Come on. Ok, who took you to the hospital?" I pleaded. I still was not getting it.

"Your Aunt Edie. I called Edie because she lived a block away, so she and her husband came to the house and took me to the hospital," she continued, letting out her longest explanation yet in our short conversation.

"Edie?! Why Edie? Where was Dad?" I asked, confused.

Was he sick? Was he out of town? I was confused.

"Edie lived a block away and it was the middle of the night," she answered, avoiding the second part of my question about my father's whereabouts that night.

Unsatisfied, I repeated my bigger question, "and where was Dad?"

"He wasn't home," she said softly.

"What do you mean 'he wasn't home,'" I retorted, "where was he?"

From her seat across the booth, she dropped her unsmiling gaze and looked at me square in the eyes, signaling to me that I had now waded into grave territory. My quiet mother only did this when she was serious.

She stared right into my eyes to let me know nonverbally, "Tread carefully, honey."

"Your father was not home, so Edie came and got me," she offered.

"It was the middle of the night. And he wasn't home?" I retorted again, now angry that my father missed out on his fatherly duty of taking his wife to the hospital to birth his baby.

"So, where was he?" I asked, truly curious.

"He was at his girlfriend Faye's apartment," my mother uttered, not wanting to tell me, but knowing I was not settling for less than the facts.

"WHAT? He had a GIRLFRIEND? And he was not home while he was married with A PREGNANT WIFE?", my anger was instant and dripped out of my mouth with my words.

She just stared across the booth at me, calmly.

I was angry at her for not being angry with me and disgusted with him, too.

Seeing her youngest daughter fume with anger must have been painful and confounding for my mother, the person who experienced her ex-husband's abandonment first-hand in real time. She did not want her daughter to re-experience what she herself had experienced. More than a decade had gone by, and she had put it out of her mind, never expecting her precocious daughter to dig up these details.

What I did not realize then is that her expressionless face was likely the best she could do to feign neutrality. She was shielding me from her deep pain and disgust at my father's behavior, masking the pain she felt, while also trying to keep me from feeling it, too. She never wanted her girls to hate their father, even if he deserved it.

"Yes, Erin, he had moved out," she exhaled.

"Was he there when I was born?" I asked, thinking for sure he showed up in time for his child's birth into this world.

"No, Erin, he was not. He came later," she said, somberly.

"So, basically, when I was born, he wasn't there, and he wasn't living with you. Which basically means I am a bastard?" I said, filled with anger at him for this familiar feeling of paternal neglect.

"No, Erin, you were not a bastard. We were married," she said calmly.

I remember saying to my mother, not realizing how the words must have hit her ears, "Ok, then, I was almost a bastard. My dad was just waiting for me to be born until he could divorce you. He wasn't even at the hospital when I was born." I was courtesy-non-bastardized.

Still young and unsure what the word meant, saying I was a "bastard" to my mother was weighty. Not only was I young, but I had no idea how much that word was attached to an avalanche of shame for Dorothy's daughter, my mother. My grandmother's abandonment made that word wicked and vile.

"No! You are NOT a bastard!! And you better not ever let your grandmother hear you say that!" my mother snapped, sternly.

"Bastard" was a word that went too far, and I stepped over the line. I knew from that moment on that she hated that word "bastard."

In the conversation that continued, I learned that my mother and father were actually separated while she was pregnant with me and raising her first two daughters on her own. He had moved out shortly after she got pregnant in March, and he began living with another woman, whom he would eventually marry (and then soon divorce).

My mother continued to work full-time at her federal government job in Tampa throughout her pregnancy with me. Lucky for her, it was a smooth, healthy pregnancy free of nausea and complications. An easy pregnancy meant she could carry on with taking her other two young children to daycare on her way to work each morning.

Other than a growing belly, her main worry was how she would go about raising not two but three babies on her own without their father.

The Sunday night my mother went into labor with me, she was at home with her then-two children, my older sisters. It was December 3rd, and this was not the wedding anniversary she dreamed of. She should have been celebrating her seventh wedding anniversary with her husband. Instead, she was alone, her husband was away with another woman, and she was on the verge of delivering a baby into this situation.

She knew what to expect given that this was not the first time she had given birth. She went through the motions of the first stages of labor on her own, dealing with the contractions as she tidied the house for her departure. Her two little girls ran around the house playing that evening before bedtime, not knowing a little sister would arrive the next day. Their mommy was about to give birth, and they were excited for a Christmas baby.

Once the contractions grew closer together and stronger, my mother called her sister-in-law, my aunt Edie, who lived a block away. Edie would be the stand-in for her brother, who abdicated his responsibilities yet again. It was a fairly quick labor, ending around one o'clock in the morning with the birth of a healthy baby girl. Trish would welcome her alone, and yet her deep, innate love for her new baby stood in stark contrast to the glaring absence of her baby's father. The aloneness of the hospital room drew her to a simple conclusion. It was time to move on.

Trish thought long and hard about how she would tell her mother, Dorothy, that she would be filing for a divorce. She would become the only of Dorothy's six daughters to be divorced, and she did not want to disappoint her mother. Trish was resolved that she could DO it, even if it would be hard. The benefit outweighed the cost.

Raising her children in a home free from his infidelities and instability was better than subjecting them to it. Growing up divorced and without their father in the home would be better for her girls than pretending this family was actually a functioning family. Her priority now was clear.

Two weeks after her baby's birth, she scooped up her three little daughters and drove them from south Florida all the way up to Maryland. She would not sit and wait around for her husband to share his plans for Christmas, nor would she subject her children to being second fiddle to his new girlfriend. She took matters into her own hands.

Her newborn baby would be properly baptized in her hometown church. Mary Blair, Trish's sister's daughter, would be her baby's godmother. They would spend Christmas with mother Dorothy and the rest of the Bryan clan in Indian Head. And she would tell Dorothy the news.

"Mother, when I get back to Florida, Ted and I are getting a divorce," my mother told my Granny. Granny knew things were not good, and Ted's absence on this trip was definitely not the first sign of their troubles.

"Just make sure you have done everything in your power to preserve your family," Dorothy told her daughter, Trish.

"Mother, believe me when I tell you that I have. Would you like me to tell you everything I've tried to do to make this marriage work?" Trish, the usually-shy daughter told her Mother.

"No, Trish, you know best if you've tried, and if you've done it, then that's good enough for me," Dorothy said, worried for her daughter, but supportive of her doing what was right for her girls.

Pursuing a better life for the four of them could only happen with a divorce, Trish told Dorothy.

Trish feared her mother being ashamed of her failure to keep a marriage together. Dorothy, to the contrary, saw strength in her daughter. Even though she saw her daughter's strength, Dorothy wanted Trish to take better care of her well-being.

Dorothy saw her daughter's disappointment in herself. She needed not to pile on and subject her to maternal disappointment. Instead, she offered support for her daughter, and encouraged her to stay strong for her girls. Being raised outside the confines of high Virginia society gave Dorothy a certain freedom. She was free to accept her daughter's imperfection, and, in fact, she was free to have a broader view of what "perfect" looked like.

Trish wanted her girls to have a better chance at relationships with men, and their father's example in marriage was definitely not giving them that chance. So, that Christmas at home in Indian Head, Trish and her three girls enjoyed their time at Mother/Granny's house. Yet, perhaps more importantly, her mother helped her set the restart button, settling her fears of reprisal and giving her courage, support, and love to start anew on her own.

Dorothy held her new baby granddaughter. She sent Trish and her three granddaughters back home to Florida just after Christmas. She did not know for sure what awaited them, but she loved them.

ERIN L. RICHMAN

18

--
A Silent Distance

I never witnessed my grandmother, Dorothy, bowing down or being reverent to anyone except for possibly a priest. Even then, the priest was reverent to her as much, if not more, as she was to them. The energetic ambitious young girl was now was a commander.

In her own way, Dorothy was not one of these women that loved men. Yes, she surely had her own way. She got along with priests as long as they didn't buck her. Priests wouldn't have sex, supposedly.

"When she found out they were having it, that really put a kink in her armor," her only son Marbury laughed.

As Marbury perceived it, he never saw Dorothy put a hand on her daughters Mary Blair or Kathleen. His sisters knew better of his propensity to exaggerate while story-telling.

"The other girls, especially Elizabeth and Josephine, my God, they really got it," Marbury bellowed.

And so it was. Dorothy was imperfect, as any human is. She was regal to some, scary to others. Her granddaughters saw her as their regal matriarch, while her grandsons perhaps experienced her majesty's ire. Her revile for her natural father made her skeptical of so many future men in her life, including her grandsons.

Her only son, then, bore the pressure of living up to his Mother's exacting standards. As a male, the bar of approval was undoubtedly higher, if unattainable altogether. Except for the celibate priests, it was unclear if any male could pass muster.

For her 13 granddaughters, however, she was a pillar of strength and resolve. Standing at a mere 5'2" at her peak, she stood tall for whatever she believed in – to men and women alike. Her command was one that her granddaughters could only wish to emulate.

"It didn't take much for her to blow up. She had to swallow her ferocity and eat it at work, but when she got home, don't get in her way," Marbury recalled.

"She'd go a week, maybe two weeks and wouldn't even speak to you if you were on her shit list. That's what they call the strong, silent treatment," as Marbury explained Dorothy's knack for the silent spurn.

"No one could compete with her, and there was no point in trying to compete with her. She would have a stack of cards for her grandchildren, the cards were always ready. Every month she'd go get cash up at the bank for the grandchildren for Christmas, their birthday, or Easter," Marbury explained of his mother's unrivalled, meticulous planning.

As her granddaughters saw it, there was a regality to her that came naturally. Maybe it was just the time period that she lived in when men and women were more proper. Women wore dresses, hats were commonplace, stockings were a daily routine, not just something you wore to the special occasion of a wedding or to a job interview. All things were much more proper during her time.

Yet and still, she seemed to easily exude a level of comportment, properness, and stature very naturally. It leaves one to wonder: Is there truly such a thing as blue bloods? Is that real? Is it really *in the blood*? For her, comportment certainly seemed effortless, unpracticed, natural, and inherently deserved. There was nothing fake about her presence.

Ironically, though Dorothy never bowed down to anyone else, she seemed – at least in her mind and in the lives of her children – to have a deep, permeating reverence to – and perhaps *fear of* – her biological family legacy.

Her heritage in the Zimmer family was known to all. Her story always lingered like oxygen in the air, but it was rarely spoken of. It didn't need to be. Its weight could be felt, even if it was not named.

Her birth story's significance stood quietly as the elephant in her life's room. Her children knew very well the story of their mother's family. They knew her real family – the Zimmers – as the "blue bloods." They, her seven children, laughed behind her back at her exacting ways and pursuit of perfection.

Dorothy's seven children were *of* the blue bloods, though they were never confused to think they belonged *among* them. Their mother, however, sat saintly atop their brood, and, in her children's mind, belonging with the blue bloods. Their mother, Dorothy, was cheated out of her core sense of belonging. Dorothy's birth story always lurked, and pushed her subconsciously in ways her drive alone could not have.

Dorothy kept a silent distance, yet stayed in tune. She had a quiet, profound respect for who the Zimmers were and what they represented, even if she could not partake or participate in that charmed life.

Who looks outside, dreams; who looks inside, awakes.
Carl Jung

She paid keen attention to her brother William's happenings from 100 miles away in Southern Maryland. Close enough to stay tuned.

Once she learned about her family's existence, she read about them and researched their comings and goings. She followed her brother, William, in his accomplishments at the University of Virginia. She clipped the full-page newspaper story about her sister Polly's wedding to Archibald Cochran.

In the Fall of 1934, she and her future-husband, Alexander, bundled up and drove the 36 miles up to College Park. Her brother, William, was there to play football with his UVA Cavaliers football against the Maryland Terps. At that time, William was a Varsity letterman on the UVA football team and played on the starting lineup. Dorothy sat inconspicuously in the stands to watch her brother. He had no idea he had another sister, much less that this stranger-sister was silently watching him play from the stands.

What went through her mind as she watched her brother from mere yards away? She must have chosen her seat carefully – close enough to see the expressions on players' faces on the sidelines, but far enough to not be noticed. Surely, she studied her brother's sweaty face and mannerisms as he paced the sideline.

Dorothy remained tuned in from her silent distance. She followed William's life and career as his career ascended. She read about him and his company, A.H. Robins, in the *Washington Post,* and clipped and saved the stories. Decades later, when his granddaughter's wedding was announced in the *Tampa Tribune,* she clipped that newspaper story as well.

She wrote her brother a sympathy letter when he had to pay a settlement for his role in the A.H. Robins class action lawsuit.

"Are you just trying to pour salt in your wound?" Marbury, Dorothy's only son, probed.

Marbury could see better than perhaps anyone how much Dorothy self-imposed her anguish. Marbury was the only one who had tried to bridge the gap between Dorothy and the Zimmers. Consequently, Marbury uniquely felt Dorothy's scorn for breaching the appearances to which she conformed.

She made annual pilgrimages to Petersburg, where she slowly cruised past 244 S. Sycamore Street but never stopped to get out of her car. She never knocked on the door. She took her children sometimes. She took her grandchildren other times. Just to look. Just to breathe their same air. And wonder, what might her life have been if…

She scheduled lunches with Lindsay Walker Hay, her biological aunt. Lindsay knew about the baby that wasn't. She met with Dorothy in person on occasion, but mostly wrote letters back and forth after Dorothy discovered more of the story. The letters continued for many years, as did the lunches, though it was a strained relationship.

Lindsay was her Aunt – her mother's sister – and she knew the real story of Dorothy's birth. She was the sister in whom Polly confided and trusted. Lindsay knew it perhaps better than anyone, even if she didn't speak openly of it.

Lindsay would be the closest Dorothy ever got to her mother, yet even she treated Dorothy with ambivalence. Dorothy could only wonder how the shapes of Lindsay's eyes looked like Polly's. Dorothy wondered if her mother was as cold and bitter as her aunt Lindsay.

Lindsay could look at Dorothy and see familiarity. Of course, she saw the square face and almond eyes of Sam, her now-dead brother-in-law. Dorothy was his spitting image. Lindsay cringed imagining what could have been and quickly trained herself out of the slightest wonderings, banishing longing from her mind as quickly as it entered.

Lindsay was cool to Dorothy, yet kept in contact with her as each year turned to a decade. She never shared anything about Dorothy with her niece and nephew, Polly and William, keeping her knowledge of their full-blood sister to herself. At some level, perhaps she felt guilty for being an accomplice in hiding her sister's pregnancy in Winter 1909. Perhaps she knew that she helped Sam hide this baby, and pushed her sister to carry on as normal. Perhaps she wondered if she played a part – even remotely – in her sister's demise.

As their interactions evolved, Dorothy followed Lindsay's lead. Lindsay did the asking. Dorothy was willing to bend to whatever Lindsay was willing to give. Little did Dorothy know, for all of Lindsay's appearance of social stature, that she herself was a struggling, divorced woman living alone, left by her ambitious husband years before. Lindsay still had the pride of a Walker-Pryor child, minus the wealth. Dorothy, however, came to want very little of Lindsay's aloof demeanor, and did not make efforts to remain in touch once she gained a fuller view of Lindsay.

Dorothy needn't learn this same pride. She possessed it herself. Yet, she could never shake the thought of what she missed out on as the child abandoned by this family of stature and legacy. It drove her to prove herself – if even only to herself – that she belonged.

Yet, her spirit was bowed by knowing she was the only abandoned child of this "fine" Virginia family. Her life – before knowing – was moving along quite nicely, but the revelations which had come to Dorothy had naturally made a profound impression on her, much to the detriment of her peace of mind.

Dorothy was fully and forever changed, especially in light of the facts she learned as to her real parents, their life and social position, and their seeming abandonment of her. What had originated as a seemingly simple request for her birth certificate had forever transformed what she knew of herself. The simple word "family" would never mean the same thing to her again. And her own social position would forevermore be compared to what she'd be cast out of at her birth.

Her real family, the Zimmers, had a legacy of leaders in the American Revolution. Her mother came from a legacy of intelligent women writers. Her mother Polly had kept her other children. Sam and Polly and their kept children carried on with their lives behind the iron gates on 244 South Sycamore Street.

Dorothy held Polly harmless for her abandonment, yet fully blamed Sam. She had furious recurring dreams of chasing Sam, with one dream in particular of her holding the steering wheel, driving the very car that ran him over and killed him on the Virginia highway outside Petersburg.

Dreams are signifiers of our deepest emotions. Indeed, as psychiatrist Carl Jung asserted in *The Meaning of Psychology for Modern Man* (1934):

> 'The dream is the small hidden door in the deepest and most intimate sanctum of the soul"

Dorothy's dreams were undoubtedly an opening into the most inner parts of her psyche, particularly as she dealt with men. This part of her psyche forever inspected men for their selfishness and potential harm. This part of her psyche filled her with infinite, searing hate for Sam, and all similarly blonde-haired, blue-eyed men with charming woo. All men were capable of deceit and ruthlessness, as Sam exhibited in abandoning Dorothy.

Sam was the villain in her life's tragedy; Polly was her once-regal, mortally-wounded sufferer, whose own life was gulped by Sam's unquenchable ambition. The story Dorothy told herself was self-protective, pitting her *good mother* against her *evil father*, and creating a conjunction of pride and shame. Pride at being part of the regal line of the good, and shame for being denied her rightful place within it by the evil Sam. This was her very own *Syzygy*, what Jung termed as the pairing of opposites.

Yet, the irony is that there was no simple answer. Polly was not simply Sam's victim. Sam was likely not pure evil. They co-constructed their tragic lives.

For Dorothy, there were no answers for her questions. There was no comfort from the interrogations that irritated her mind; no itch for what scratched at her. She had difficulty understanding why her mother would consent to her abandonment. She yearned deeply in her core to control the chaos that resulted from being born a despised and disposed baby.

It was as if Dorothy was the embodiment of the very words Jung wrote. Coincidentally, he wrote these very words during the precise time she was uncovering the shocking details of her birth story.

Again, from Carl Jung in 1934:

> "In allem Chaos ist Kosmos und in aller Unordnung geheime Ordnung."

Translated, Jung says:

"In all chaos there is a cosmos, in all disorder a secret order."

Sam and Polly's abandonment of her – after they were married – made no sense to her. Having more babies and never coming back for her, that made no sense to her either. It was a mistake. It was wrong, disordered.

But if Jung was right, was there an order that coexisted – even superseded – this disorder? If he was right, there was an order to this disorder; a secret, less visible order.

In fact, Dorothy, herself, was the secret order.

She bore the weight of the secret, once born only by her now-dead mother.

Dorothy's syzygy yielded mystifying, complicated expressions of pride and shame about her history.

On the one hand, Dorothy possessed a great dignity in her self-comportment and in her children, perhaps at knowing she came from such prominence. Yet, on the other hand, she once wrote a letter of apology to her never-met brother, William, though she herself had done nothing to earn William an apology. In her self-imposed embarrassment, she had been compelled to profess apology and disappointment to

William after her son's uninvited, surprise visit to William at his office in Richmond.

Dorothy's only son Marbury was raised with a compelling desire for truth and good, even when it was unpleasant. He cared not for the pleasantries and burdens of propriety, much like his mother's cousin, Dorsey Waters.

By his own volition at age 16, Marbury set out to right the wrongs done unto his mother. Marbury told no one of his plan. He just did it. He had six sisters, who he knew would blab if he mentioned a word of it. He kept his plan to himself.

He set out from D.C. alone, before there were cell phones or pagers, with one purpose on his mind: To meet his mother's brother. He would see the face that went with the name – W.L. Zimmer – that was neatly carved into the curbside granite at 244 South Sycamore Street, the stately old mansion that he'd seen from his mother's car just a few weeks earlier.

"One Friday – it was October by then – I got on the train at Union Station, and I went to Richmond. When I got there, I called him [William] from a pay phone on the street, introduced myself, and told him I was coming up," Marbury recounted.

"He told me to come on up to his office and invited me in, where we talked. He was friendly enough," Marbury said with a lilt in his voice, recounting his surprise that a Zimmer man would be welcoming and friendly to him.

Marbury is still to this day just as rambunctious and opinionated, so this should have been no surprise for his character, especially to his mother. Marbury's one and only meeting with William, his uncle, was a friendly meeting. From the scars of the Zimmers' rejection of her at age 21, Dorothy suspected that Marbury's visit also would be met with demeaning scorn.

Marbury asked William, with a hint of protest directed at William, "do you even know who your sister is?"

William had to be stunned at this young man's audacity and fervor, yet he was friendly to him. Here was this dark-eyed, dark haired young man, Marbury, sitting across from him in his office, claiming to be his sister's son. He only knew of ONE sister – he was the youngest of two, not the youngest of three.

Here sat this young man, proudly asserting himself on behalf of his mother. William had to be both amazed and unsure what to say. "He was nice enough," Marbury recalled of tenor of the visit.

"I would believe she's my father's daughter, but not my mother's. My mother would have never done that," William retorted.

Apparently, he and his lost sister had this in common, too – a sympathy for their mother, Polly. And they shared the belief that their father was capable of moral transgressions, including betrayal of his wife and family. Mother Polly, however, was pure and wholesome always. For entirely different reasons, they placed Polly on a pedestal as the purest, most innocent of mothers, clinging to a myth of who they wanted to believe she was.

Whatever William thought of Marbury's claims, he conceded that he certainly believed some part of it. Surely, their physical likeness made this stranger from Maryland seem less crazy. For William to even entertain Marbury's presence in his private office and give him even two minutes of his busy schedule, he must have accepted that Marbury *could be* his relative.

From a distance, Dorothy apologized to William for her son's visit. In her letter, she apologized to William for Marbury's behavior, and also shared that Marbury had a terrible car accident shortly after the visit. Dorothy assured William a visit would never happen again. Dorothy's apology letter was a symbol of her dignity and a very open demonstration of her own competence with propriety. And a feat of mental gymnastics.

Dorothy performing the role as the upholder of propriety was quite the irony. This very person, Dorothy, wholly created amid improprieties and forever-stained from propriety's run-off, became the enforcer of propriety. As great child psychologists say, only a person who starts with a basic sense of pride and self-possession would be capable of experiencing true embarrassment.

Or, perhaps, the apology for Marbury's visit was simply an excuse to reach out to her brother. Marbury's visit to William gave her a defined, acceptable purpose for reaching out. Even if she shrouded her desire for contact with an apology, she would still be able to count it among the few contacts she would ever have with her brother.

Perhaps in another life, Marbury would have been praised for his bravery and determination. Perhaps his sincere desire to bring respect and reunion for his mother would have been celebrated. Indeed, she very much cultivated his curiosity and sympathy when she physically drove him up to the doorstep of 244 South Sycamore Street on one of her many treks to Petersburg. Marbury was the lone person besides Dr. Lawrence who would ever challenge a Zimmer over Dorothy's abandonment.

Marbury insisted then and to this day that he never meant to cause harm, as his true intent was only to bring them together. As he saw it, all his mother longed for and thought about was this family. He thought, as her only son, he would make it happen and be the bridge. He would finally connect them.

Dorothy couldn't easily forgive her son for breaking the code of propriety and interfering with the Zimmers. But why? Was it out of respect? Self-respect?

Dorothy sent William more letters when his company, A.H. Robins, was experiencing legal difficulties. He, the CEO, was facing scrutiny as a result of the Dalkon Shield IUD scandal. She expressed her sorrow at his misfortune, though he wasn't experiencing misfortune at all. He died a wealthy man.

It is noteworthy that this woman who commanded deep and profound respect from her peers, her children, and grandchildren, still held a place for this family that rejected her, giving them reverence. She was regal and revered in her own right.

Maybe it was the mystery and the unknown – what she didn't get, and what she missed out on – that kept her tuned in from afar.

OF MARY BLAIR DESTINY

19

--
Praise the Lord and Pass the Ammunition – LOVE!

    Rejection pierced Dorothy. Her life was advancing happily until the "disruption" at age 21. She never understood how her mother Polly could abandon her as an infant, unless she believed she had died in childbirth. There was no other way to comprehend it but to blame Sam for it. Rejection was an impossible pill for Dorothy to swallow – both times it happened.

    First, when learning of Sam and Polly's abandonment of her at birth, she attached to the belief that Polly was not to blame. Later, when her Zimmer relatives refused to accept her, she fought back and hired an investigator to prove her lineage to them. When she could not convince them herself discretely and personally, she forced them to acknowledge the facts in recorded deed. Sadly, shame and secrecy prevented her from ever knowing any kindness from Sam and Polly's offspring.

    Cousin Dorsey's unconditional acceptance – and light-hearted teasing – soothed her wounds. His would be the only salve she ever received from any relative. Dorsey gave Dorothy lifelong friendship, and a single connection to her family history that she cherished.

> Honey, you complain about not hearing from me, you should know by now that I am not very demonstrative, except when I've had a drink or two. You know that I care a lot for you and I don't see how calling you up or writing to you can make any possible difference in our relationship. You will have to realize that your only relative, who will admit it, is a peculiar sort of a cuss and will have to be taken just as is. Aunt Mad sends her regards.
>
> Your Cousin
>
> Dorsey

The memories of rejection did not stop her from publicly claiming her real name and demonstrating commitment to *her truth*, even if her birth family would never share it with her. Rejection did not stop her from vigilantly pursuing the truth of her birth story. Rejection did not stop her from boldly claiming her birth name alongside her given name:

Dorothy Hardy Bryan nèe Mary Blair Zimmer

She named her parents as "Samuel W. and Polly Zimmer of Petersburg, VA" in her 1937 marriage announcement and in her official obituary in 1997. She also had her birth name stamped on her gravestone for perpetuity, too. Though she surrendered to the fact that her birth family would never accept her, she never surrendered claim to her birth right once she knew it.

She remained close with her "foster" parents, George and Bertha Hardy. They helped her get started after she was married, lived with her family when they were elderly, and were proud grandparents to her seven children. They stayed by Dorothy's side throughout their lives.

Always fierce and standing proud, Dorothy was a vanguard amongst women of her generation. She persisted in every one of the 88 years she lived. Upon learning she actually *had siblings*, but then accepting she would never know them, she used her power to *create* the family she longed for, not to wallow in self-pity.

It took nearly half of her twenties, but she got herself back on track. She created the love and bonding she yearned for herself. The births of her "Magnificent Seven" children gave her the family she so craved. Finally, she could move beyond the rejection.

Her seven knew her as a strict and exacting matriarch; she was fierce as she was resilient. Yet, their mother created a fierce and resilient bond of love amongst the seven – one that she herself was never so fortunate to know as a sibling. Her children would never know the seclusion, or not belonging, for they always would belong to each other.

Dorothy resolutely pushed her only son, Marbury, when he literally broke. Marbury was split and busted in half by violent car accident at age 17, nearly killed and his survival in question. Even though his body would never be the same after his car accident, she didn't tolerate any of his melancholy, for there was reason to remain resilient.

"You pick yourself up, dust yourself off, hold your head high, and you keep your feet moving," was a familiar refrain of Dorothy's, said with her southern Maryland cadence and inflection.

"You can do this, Marbury. Now get yourself moving," he could hear her declare in his mind long after she uttered the words.

As certain as she was of Marbury's resilience, Dorothy was just as certain of her father Sam's responsibility for her abandonment and mother Polly's suffering. Handsome, charming men forever became suspects to her, needing to be put in check for their scurrilous, selfish intentions with women. Men were prone to corruptness, except for the chosen few in the eyes of Dorothy. In the eyes of her young granddaughters, Dorothy's strength with men seemed feminist-avant-garde, yet it was quite possibly her shield guarding her vulnerability, protecting her from any potential repeat pain she felt Sam alone had dealt her. It may well have shielded her from the joys of vulnerability, too.

In her devout Catholic faith, she found reprieve, practicing gratitude for her blessed life and pleading mercy for others. She sent cards every season, handwritten and closed with her trademark confident, cursive, authoritative penmanship,

God Bless you!
Love,
Granny

Her behests were sincere. She had no control in the fate she was born into, yet she grounded herself in faith deeply and daily, psychologically and spiritually.

"Take care of your Mother, you'll never have another," she first wrote to me in a birthday card when I was a teen.

Dorothy always knew her mother Polly died young. Though she had no definitive evidence for it, she steadfastly believed Polly died so young from her own melancholy. She would never know Polly in life, yet she would live life wondering what happened to cause her mother to abandon her as an infant. She would never get that answer.

Yet, it was superb, sublime triumph of the human spirit that she, Dorothy, would have a son – her only son – who persisted through his own pain and melancholy – the same pain and melancholy that consumed her own mother.

Marbury's body was broken, yet he persisted. Physically, he embodied his mother's split family, and his survival mirrored his mother's. His resilience was the product of her drilling, fierce bonds forged with his siblings, and loyal love from his wife, Gloria.

To be sure, there was nothing romantic about Dorothy and Marbury's shared tragedies. Because of them, undoubtedly, life was more difficult, even painful. And their lives had both visible and hidden scars.

Scars hidden in secret are indeed some of the most difficult to overcome. Yet, great healing is possible when hidden scars are revealed. In claiming her birthname for herself and her daughter, Dorothy exposed her scars and created a path for healing.

Indeed, Mary Blair, Dorothy's second eldest daughter and namesake, became a torchbearer of her mother's healing. Independent in her own right, Mary Blair married a handsome young beau, John, and forged her own path to motherhood with eight children of her own.

Like her brother Marbury, Mary Blair became the physical embodiment of her mother, yet her life embodied her mother's quest for a whole, complete family unit. Mary Blair cultivated a family where belonging and love existed without question. Mary Blair's motherhood was defined by unconditional love and acceptance as non-negotiables. She unconsciously transformed the legacy of her grandparents' rejection and her Mother's scars.

Whereas Dorothy's path was born from deep scars of rejection, Mary Blair's pursuit of love and family was composed from a *tabula rasa*. She was liberated of her mother's bindings. Yet, like Marbury, she shared fierce bonds with her siblings. Despite being whisked away from her mother by a dashing beau at a mere 17 years old, Mary Blair's rich and fertile life was the realization of what Dorothy hoped for from her own mother, Polly, but never attained.

Marbury and Mary Blair shared their Mother's unconscious burdens, in both dark and light. They outdid the legacies they were handed. Marbury overcame the melancholy that consumed his mother's mother. Mary Blair overcame bindings of motherhood and forged her own path. Unsurprisingly, among the magnificent seven of Dorothy's brood, the two were among the most "Alpha" children to their Alpha mother.

July 10, 1989

Dear Mary Blair, John, et al:

Praise the Lord and Pass the Ammunition! You praised the Lord and passed the ammunition - L O V E! The celebration you planned and participated in, for my eightieth birthday was brimming over with love. Venistis, Vidistis, Vicistis!

I shall not attempt to thank each and everyone individually - I do not know who did what, however, I do know that it all came together in such a superb manner that it is almost unbelievable. But then, on the other hand, it was the seven BRYAN adult children, with cooperation of their spouses, children and friends, who engineered the events. Need I say more? I am proud of you, and thankful to God that He has blessed me with a wonderful family.

I am happy that, in the conniving, you were brought together over a period of so many months, by the various channels of communication - hopefully, you will continue to keep in touch.

Beginning the joyful occasion with Holy Mass was most appropriate. I treasure the Apostolic Blessing of Pope John Paul II.

The party was the most enjoyable ever - it surpassed my retirement party. Your expressions of appreciation were more than I deserve. I accept them with gratitude, and feel that this is a new beginning (I might make it to a hundred), with the past a closed book except for the good times.

For your love, your talents, your resources, your time, and your presence, I thank all of you.

May the blessings of God's love be with you always.

Love,

Mother/Granny
Mother/Granny

PS: Pardon the typewritten letter -
I value your eyesight.

We have long-defined our family in terms of what Dorothy, our Mother/Granny, did to create it. She, alone, created this circle of 'family.' She created a very big family, indeed. While Marbury embodied her split family of origin, Dorothy's daughter, Mary Blair, was the physical embodiment of her adult quest for a complete family.

Mary Blair carried her Mother's torch not only in name, but in procreation. Mary Blair would create her own robust branch on the family tree, complete with eight children and another Mary Blair of her own to add to the line of Mary Blairs that came before them. Marbury and Mary Blair, to no one's surprise, as Dot's progeny, would be her personal forces of nature.

We had big family reunions. We had big weddings as family reunions. Dot was always there at the helm. There was Sis' wedding. Then, Mary Blair & John when they renewed wedding vows. Jimmy's wedding to Cheryl. Teri's wedding. Michael's wedding. Pete's wedding. Sharon's wedding. Mark's wedding. Becky's wedding. Marcy's wedding. Aunt Jo's remarriage. Dan and Dottie's 25th wedding vows renewal. Reina's Quinceañera.

Dorothy was present for our graduations and weddings, coming all the way to Florida from Maryland to see her grandchildren's rites of passage.

We had big birthday parties for her – at her 75th and 80th birthdays. We all gathered to honor and roast her. And her sons-in-law gathered to dance with her.

We gathered at her hospital bedside just eight years later.

We gathered again at a big funeral and wake a few weeks later.

We gathered in reunion to honor her 95th just outside of Asheville, North Carolina, where she spent her 1937 honeymoon exploring the mountains' beauty. We climbed Chimney Rock just as she had. We roasted her though she would not be there to enjoy it in the flesh.

We were blessed with knowing we were always part of something larger. We had cousins everywhere. Dot's DNA was present from sea to shining sea, from Florida to California.

We were family. And Catholic Mass was always part of our gatherings, as Granny would think it incomplete otherwise. Whether wedding, baptism, or funeral, Mass was a necessary ingredient in the order of events.

In any case, Sam died just one month before my grandmother traveled to Petersburg to find him. She never did meet him. Their paths did not cross by a small matter of days. His final accident did him in for good, and freed her from his "first accident."

Never meeting Sam was both tragic and fortunate. Tragic in that she was so close to meeting her natural father, but this was also fortunate because what would she actually say or resolve by looking into the man's eyes who surrendered her and never came back?

Facing him in person would have only made the wound deeper. Not meeting Sam would become the most unlikely good fortune, and quite likely helped her wounds heal faster and allowed her to move on with her life sooner. Not meeting him led to her getting married sooner, having her seven children precisely when she did.

Had her father lived, and not been killed weeks before she learned about him, she certainly would have met him. What would have come from that meeting is all of that would have been delayed, and possibly her life course and ours – would be completely different.

Is this destiny, then?

Her unfulfilled closure changed the narrative of her life.

Judgment of doing for appearances and redemption was denied. Instead, she embodied individual self-determination. She did what her mother could not.

The fact that at every step — the painful irony of the adage "one month amidst a smooth sea doesn't make a good sailor" — she was not daunted by a setback. It worked in her favor to have this "lacking" because she created the lives of nearly 100 people.

Had baby Dorothy not been abandoned, she would have been raised as a Mary Blair and raised by a depressed mother who shared her name. She would have been raised by a mother who endured a baby dying and endured her sister's suicide-murder. She would have been part of that family who suffered grave loss. Instead, Dorothy was spared that misery.

Instead of stepping on a banana peel, she was stepping in a pot of gold with Mother B. She could have been a victim, feeling denied, but she was raised amidst love and possibility.

Instead, she was raised by the people who *chose* her – people who saw potential in her, not *lost potential* in her. Instead of an absence, she had an abundance. She turned setback into gained resilience.

The unknown and the unknowable – these were at the core of Dorothy's allure with the Zimmers. Yet and still, fully known is the fact that her children and grandchildren's very existence *depended* upon her being abandoned and given away. Many lives' existence depended upon her enduring the pain of rejection and proceeding in living her own life.

Like a mountain that cannot see its own height from afar, her destiny – and our destiny – was fulfilled in her repair of her void. She filled in her void with the actual family, love, and belonging she longed for. We are the result of her resilience and might. Our gratitude can never repay the debt we owe to her.

She pursued love and family for herself, in her own way, on her own terms. She fulfilled a more noble destiny than either her mother or father, in their tragically foreclosed lives. Fatefully, perhaps, they never achieved true fulfillment after they abandoned her, and life ended shockingly early for both. For them, abandoning her may also have been a fateful decision, perhaps a *fatal* one.

Dorothy said in her final days of life, "I've lived a long, full life and have nothing left to achieve on this Earth."

"I am good with it. I've gotten bonus years," she said to me of her life when she met its end.

"Take care of your mother. She's the only one you've got," were the last words my Granny spoke to me, a familiar, loving refrain.

"Be good to your mother. Take care of her," my grandmother instructed me during our last conversation.

"Your mother is strong and she won't tell you, but she wants you home, you know," she looked at me with a half-smile, as if breaking difficult news to me from her deathbed. She knew I was at the beginning of my romantic educational journey to the University of Georgia, three hundred miles from home.

Dorothy, once an infant abandoned by her own parents at the beginning of her life, now laid before me at the end of her life, teaching me about mothers and love and loyalty.

Her body was ready to leave this world just a few days later. She was surrounded by love and touched by the many hands of and enveloped in the family she created as she took her last breath.

Dorothy's hospital room was eerily quiet, and its lights very dimly lit in that Fall midnight, as we all held each other's hands and held her body. It was dark, and we were all crowded in together around her bed, as she lay unconscious. Nearly 30 of us – Dorothy's children and grandchildren -- gathered to bid our matriarch farewell.

Ours is a story of strength and resilience in the struggle for love and happiness, despite *this world being a 'wilderness o' woe,' as the hymn says*. And atop the wilderness, stood our fierce matriarch, born and orphaned; dying yet surrounded in love and belonging, held by her only son.

We prayed the Rosary, saying Hail Mary's for her.

We stood in silence together, at peace with letting her go.

Dorothy's breathing slowed. Her heart beat became faint.

Marbury whispered, over and over, in her right ear, leaning over her and perched at her shoulder.

"Polly is waiting, go to Polly, go be with Polly now, Mother. Go on now. We love you, Mother," Marbury whispered, in a near-chant, over and over again.

We all stood silently behind Marbury, patiently and securely.

Marbury gave her permission to go, and freed Dorothy's soul to go find her mother's again.

Everything about her fierce, long life ultimately released us all. And, now, she and Polly were releasing, too.

Dorothy lay there motionless, laying in the arms of her own children and grandchildren who loved her.

And her heart stopped. The heart break would cease.

OF MARY BLAIR DESTINY

The Lord is my shepherd; I shall not want.

He maketh me to lie down in green pastures; he leadeth me beside the still waters.

He restoreth my soul: he leadeth me in the paths of righteousness for his name's sake.

Yea, though I walk through the valley of the shadow of death; I will fear no evil: for thou art with me; thy rod and thy staff they comfort me.

Thou preparest a table before me in the presence of mine enemies; thou anointest my head with oil; my cup runneth over.

Surely goodness and mercy shall follow me all the days of my life; and I will dwell in the house of the Lord forever.

Psalm 23:4

Dorothy's Forgiveness

I am here now –
Ah, afterlife.
With all, I am one,
Split apart from none.

But you?

How did YOU
Get in here
What or who
Did you do
To avoid
Burning Hell?
I ordered it so
More than once I recall.
Burn in Hell, you BASTARD!
Surely the heat would get you.

But now –

What is this?
It is bliss
I am one with you
And with them too
So I get to see
How even you can be
Loving and charming
And oh so fatherly
Belonging, happy

What is this happening?
This – yes this! – it must be...
How my seven felt toward me
Love and life
Eternally
I am free
To thank you

But now –
From Dorothy.

ERIN L. RICHMAN

20

--
Venisti! Vidisti! Vicisti!

As Dorothy's granddaughter, I set out on a quest many years ago to know her better. In the hot days of my own pregnancy with my first daughter, I began searching online scouring names, pictures, and records all over the internet. I did not know what I was looking for, other than I knew I wanted to know more about what happened to her and who exactly "the Zimmers" were.

I was afraid to ask my mother, as I was already too familiar with these family landmines. "The Zimmers" was a phrase said with fear and reverence, almost like saying "The Windsors" when speaking about the royal family. It was a "look-but-do-not-touch" topic. "Illegitimate" babies, shame-filled family secrets, and any curious questions on these topics were met with a glare, a stiff signal: STOP.

I wanted to know my grandmother's full, true story. I wanted to know how and why it stamped her so profoundly. I had no idea who her parents were or what became of them. Without anyone knowing what I was doing, I began my own research to seek the truth.

I pored through census records, new and old newspaper articles, and society happenings in Petersburg, Virginia, spanning many decades. I started with the one name I knew – Zimmer – in the state I knew from where they came – Virginia.

I made amazing discoveries about relatives – both living and passed. I was most stunned that I found names – names of real-life people who were actually still alive and directly connected to the old Zimmer family.

My grandmother had been deceased by well over a decade by the time I was pregnant with my own child. I did not know what I would find when I started searching for records from her birth and her family of origin. I did not know she was born in Washington, D.C., just steps from where I obtained a marriage license.

I had no idea her parents met at the University of Virginia, the same university I seriously considered for my own graduate education. I had no idea they got married five months before she was born in D.C., as I'd always assumed they were not married when she was born.

I was stunned to learn she had a full brother and sister. I found chronicles of their lives in many forms: Coming out balls, wedding announcements, summer travels to Europe, visits to Virginia from various Zimmer relatives.

Polly Zimmer Cochran and William Zimmer were my Granny's full sister and brother. Though Granny corresponded with William, she never spoke with nor met him nor her sister. They never knew what her face looked like, that she was Sam's clone.

Marbury would be the only person in our family to have come close when he brazenly visited William at his A.H. Robins office in Richmond in Fall 1962. William received Marbury just before Marbury's tragic car accident a few weeks later.

What I did not have from my own research was my Granny's story from those who knew her up close. I wanted to hear from my uncle, aunts, and my own Mother about my Granny's story.

These questions for my uncle and aunts would lead to more questions and answers I couldn't possibly expect. Understanding Polly, Sam, Dorothy, and our family's story taught me more than I ever imagined.

Two people have given up a baby in my family (that I know of). Both babies were given up because they weren't born under social norms of the day. One baby, however, could have been provided for, had two parents, married, had a home, had social means and financial means to survive.

I restarted this journey with family by first talking to my cousin, Marcy, who grew up a few houses away from our grandmother, Dorothy, and was the daughter of my only uncle, Marbury. She would be the first family member to either grant me permission to move forward, or shut me down.

Thankfully, she didn't shut me down.

My own research yielded every relic of what might be left behind from a person's earthly existence.

I analyzed maps of old D.C. I looked for streets that existed before there were paved roads.

I searched for houses no longer standing and streets in D.C. that have been replaced by highways. I read 100-year-old newspaper articles, looking into the social lives and political movements of Polly and Sam. I read glorious wedding announcements and quietly tragic obituaries.

I scanned ships' registries, noting my relatives' global travels in the age before airplane travel.

I scoured U.S. Census records, seeing who lived with whom, and where, and when they merged and split homes.

I marveled at the elegant penmanship in the signatures on marriage certificates. And I read the formal eloquence in letters shared back and forth between Dorothy and her discovered family.

I confirmed birth certificates, gasped at death certificates, and solemnly studied the words on old tombstones.

Never before in my life have I felt so connected to a set of ancestors for an area of the country. I love history – any history – family history, American history, and post-Civil War history, old furniture, historical photographs, antique items.

My paternal grandfather Charlie from Philadelphia – I never quite connected with his story except that so many Richman people lived in his hometown Philadelphia. There was always something hazy about him, so my connection to his branch of the family tree was never compelling.

My paternal grandmother, Cynthia Roberts, from Willacoochee Georgia, was colorful, but I never quite connected with her story of despair in the Great Depression. She fled from South Georgia and never returned, so there was not much romantic to connect to her roots either.

For 48 hours I stayed in a rented hotel room in Williamsburg, Virginia. Somewhat accidentally, I discovered that the drive between Williamsburg and Petersburg was history lesson in itself. The hour-long drive along dark, two-lane roads stimulated my mind to wonder what happened in the centuries before along those same roads and on the plantations by which I was passing.

The two-lane road runs through old plantations – and more plantations. Beautiful trees, grassy hills, time-worn rocks, and fenced acreage. Rolling hills, converted railroad track to bike trail running alongside double-yellow-lined pavement. My contemplations were easily transformed into freshly written words as I weaved through history and scenery. There was beauty and solemnity in those darkened woods of old Virginia.

As my days of research ended and I drove through the darkened woods holding secrets to Virginia's past, I could imagine the blackness along the highway road where Sam's life ended.

With my own pupils fully dilated to see in the night, it seemed so inexplicable to me that Sam would have walked into the bright headlights of an oncoming car – accidentally. Would this man – a man who took such careful steps to preserve his standing – not be so careful to protect his actual life? And if it was an accident, how crazily ironic that an accident such as this would determine the end of his otherwise carefully-scripted life. This accident, unlike Polly's pregnancy, was one that money and status could not mitigate for him.

In Virginia, I relished imagining my great-grandparents living and breathing and walking along the same sidewalks with me, and along with towering figures in American history such as Madison, Jefferson, and Henry. I could easily imagine my grandmother, her husband, and her children riding in their 1960 sedan, barreling down the two-lane roads that connect their small southern Maryland town to colonial, Northern Virginia. I could picture them crossing the same 2-lane postwar bridge across the Potomac and James Rivers. And winding through the piney woods of Virginia just to do drive-bys of their "stranger-relatives" in Petersburg.

No doubt, knowing her penchant for intentionality, she visited Petersburg in the summer on purpose - to visit her mother's grave on the anniversary of her death. And she likely talked her husband's ear off the whole way down. Marbury learned a lot from his mother just sitting in the backseat on those treks to Petersburg.

I picture them pulling up to the curb on S. Sycamore Street, the same curb marked by a large block of beautifully inscripted granite, "WL Zimmer," as in, the namesake of her brother William Louis Zimmer. Her brother, the A.H. Robins CEO; Her brother, the businessman-lawyer who mixed with the likes of future-supreme court justice, Petersburg's own Louis F. Powell.

I feel freedom in physically connecting to this place. I feel grounded imagining more than just me driving up and down the road making memories. Making good memories while driving up and down roads - roads you know your grandparents, their grandparents, and their parents also drove down - the same roads having front seat conversations by dashboard light - that is freeing. It is freeing to know I am one speck in a long, dynamic and "accidental" history, and that my forebears' souls are watching over me as I traverse their haunting grounds.

I feel connected. Grounded by the purpose of my ancestors, I am less alone in my struggle for love and happiness in this world.

I feel liberated. My grandmother's resilience and strength throughout having her birthright rejected, while demeaned by money, frees me to be fiercely resilient myself.

Nothing could prepare me for the stories – the complex, *un-simple* lives – of these relatives. What we nostalgically beckon to be a "simpler" time was really only simpler on the surface. Life has always been messy and complicated.

They still had petty squabbles, annoyance at social posturing, buried secrets, hushed scandals, and perpetual struggles to be happy. My relatives struggled for belonging and love, and some never were resolved in believing they had it.

For the flaws she surely had, I easily forgive my grandmother, Dorothy. For her temper, her strictness, her tantrums (I never witnessed), I can empathize with her. To expect perfection from any human being is naïve and impractical.

She, as everyone, was worn by the bruises of her very existence. The bright, industrious girl would discover the painful truth of her life and be double-stung by denial and disowning. Nevertheless, she grew into a strong, industrious woman who balanced being Mother to her seven children with her civil service career and being Choir Director and Organist at church. She veiled her pain of rejection with thick sheathings of productivity and piousness.

She, as very few could do, resolved to persevere. She pursued love even though it did not rescue her upon her entry to this world. She built a family of her own, even though her own family delivered the searing pain of not acknowledging her.

Since her death, I have had many conversations with my Granny. Whether it is purely a figment of my imagination, or the essence of Dorothy's spirit truly hearing me, I think of her when I could use good luck, when I need strength, and when I am short on faith. Until recently, I had no idea how I was calling upon exactly the right person for these reinforcements.

Her luck delivered her, when she had no parents claiming her, to a couple that truly loved her, that CHOSE her. Her luck found her supported by the arms of a woman who had all the room in the world to love a baby. Her luck delivered her to a doctor who saved her from a black market of baby-selling. Her luck delivered her.

Her strength carried her when her world was rocked. Her strength gave her the courage to carry on and bear seven children. Her strength gave her the courage to support her son through his life-altering accident. It allowed her to accept and love her daughter through a failed marriage and financial struggles. Her strength carried her.

Her faith held her when she might break. Her faith grounded her children and grandchildren in a common value for love, family, virtue, and justice. Her faith gave her familiarity when her world turned upside down and gave her a script for life's greater purpose.

Knowing her now, and having vicariously experienced the details of her lived story, she is more human to me. Yet, I love her even more, and my hope is that she will feel this love eternally from me and the many others who never knew her. An arbor of strength, loyalty, and truth, her legacy rises within each of us.

ERIN L. RICHMAN

How I Want to Tell You, Granny!

I am Joyful and free
At these discoveries

Number eighteen
Your proud progeny

On behalf of you
– Yet impossibly –

I scaled our tree
Proudly laid claim

To roots
between
branches
he split

To make our destiny.

I suspect this is all your doing
Whether by your genes or spirit

Or both?

I have the mind of a sleuth
For which I credit you alone.

Poring over pages –
Digital – this century

Only to find that
You'd already beaten me

Two Motherhoods –
1909,
then fast forward
one century

One denied by shame
One claiming openly.

1931 you,
2019 me.
We fixed this,
Together.

Because… your records
Impeccable!
Your details,
Uncanny!

So, now,
Please feel –
from me –
Devoted
Loyalty
Undying
Respect
And deep
Deep empathy.

Always you were strong
Yet until now
I could not see –
Brilliance Resilience Radiance

Vulnerability.

Yes, I have your
Audacity.

With love to you,
My dearest Granny.

Venisti! Vidisti! Vicisti!

21

--
Summoning My Grandmother's Gumption

As I set out on the Mary Blair Project, I knew I could not proceed without permission. Over the years of on-and-off research, my sleuthing was done in private, without anyone really knowing besides my spouse. What I found satisfied my own personal curiosities. The couple of times I shared details with my mother, she bristled at my finding names of people who were her "Zimmer" relatives. As such, she also never failed to remind me that Granny certainly would not condone me contacting these people.

She made it clear that I was to never cross that line. Looking at pictures online was one thing. She knew her curious daughter was tempted to reach out, so she admonished me pre-emptively.

If I was to go further in my research of Granny's story, I needed the blessing of my mother first. I needed her six siblings' blessings, too. Or, I bargained, at the very least, I needed my Uncle Marbury's blessing. I had a vision, and I wanted to see it come to fruition.

I figured if I had both my mother's blessing and her brother's, they could convince the other five that my touching this story was okay. If Marbury and Trish were not okay with it, none of the others would be either. All these old rocks would get turned over and old landmines would be exposed, and I couldn't risk an army of relatives being mad at me for eternity.

I could have started with my mother, but I was too afraid to ask her outright, so I decided to start by calling my cousin Marcy. She is slightly older than me and is Uncle Marbury's eldest daughter. Marcy was also very close to our Granny, and she still lived close to her parents, so I knew she would be a good gauge.

Marcy had no idea why I wanted to talk to her out of the blue like this, but she accepted my mystery invitation to chat on the phone. All I wanted to glean from her is whether, in her opinion, me approaching and asking questions of her father would be too upsetting. Marbury had always been the family historian in addition to being one of its most colorful personalities. If it was too much and too dangerous to touch, I would just stop. I would not touch it.

--

Calling Cousin Marcy – October 31

I called Marcy at work. She didn't know about my mom's ordeal. She said her dad knows a lot about Granny's story. I explained to her what I want to do, to explore Granny's story, and honor her. She listened quietly as I told her I wanted to talk to her dad, Marbury, to learn more.

"You don't want to get yourself sued, Erin," Marcy, ever-the-cautious-eldest cautioned.

"I won't," I said, and I believed it, though I am pretty sure Marcy thought I was crazy. I was known for being the cavalier.

"If you talk to my dad, be prepared for a long conversation," she said, trying to give me full warning.

"Sis knows a lot, too, she might be easier," as she continued to gently encourage me not to talk to her father.

Marcy was skeptical, if not confused about why I would want to do this. And she reminded me that Granny signed an agreement that forbid her from ever contacting the Zimmers and from making her story public. She was concerned I might violate the agreement Granny had made back in 1935.

"Is your Mother okay with this? Have you talked to her?" Marcy wisely probed.

"I wanted to talk to you first. I am talking to my mom, too, and will surely get her permission. If she is good with it, I will reach out to your dad, but I wanted to talk to you first to see if you even thought this was something he'd entertain – talking to me," I shared my thinking with her.

"Yes, he would probably love nothing more than to talk your ear off," Marcy said as she cautiously expressed approval.

She then mentioned a name, "Dorsey Waters. He was a cousin of Granny's or something. It was a weird thing, like 'Right place at right time'. She crossed paths with him by some strange twist of fate."

"People in Granny's life at that time were somehow connected to the Zimmers," and that was the extent of what Marcy shared, outside of granting approval to approach her father.

This only piqued my curiosity more.

Three Days Later – Mom's Blessing

I talked to my mom about a book topic and about possibly talking to her brother, my uncle Marbury, aka holder of family history.

"What's your book about, Erin?" she asked, with a hint of humored suspicion in her question.

"Historical fiction," I said.

"Uh huh," she mumbled, half-suspicious.

Silence.

Before I knew any real details, I planned to write the story as fiction. As it turned out, the truth was too strange to be fiction.

"And what's your book about?" she prodded me further.

"The struggle for love and happiness in this life. *The pursuit*. The pursuit of love and happiness in this life," I answered.

"Uh-huh. And who's in this book?" she asked, still following her suspicion, yet on the verge of giggles.

"Four generations of women," I reply.

Laughter.

"I knew it. What are these four women's names?" my mother asked me.

"Mom, I said they're fictional."

"Uh-huh. What are the names, Erin?" she pushed on.

"Holly Calker." I said instead of Polly Walker.

Laughing, "Erin! Richman!"

"Go on." In typical mom fashion, she was intrigued by the naughtiness.

"Chorothy Tardy," I say, instead of Dorothy Hardy.

"Anna Cryin." I say instead of Anna Bryan.

"Anna Cryin??? Huh? And who's Chorothy?"

"Mom, those are fake names. DOROTHY HARDY. ANNA BRYAN."

"Ohhh. Right. Ok."

"So, who's the fourth?" she asks.

"Me." I say.

"Oh. And what do these women's stories have to do with each other? How are you going to connect them?" Mom asks.

"They were all pursuing a better life. Polly was pursuing love in Sam and likely her baby, but the baby was stripped from her, and, later a second baby was also. She died from the sadness," I start.

"Dorothy was pursuing the love and happiness of family when she was seeking her birth family. When they rejected her, she created it in her own seven children she birthed between age 30 and 40. What she didn't find, she created for herself. Ironically, she would watch the same "thing" that tormented her biological mother happen again in her own children."

"You can leave that part out," Mom admonished me.

"And then, as Dorothy's daughter pursued happiness and better life in getting a divorce, Dorothy let her know she didn't approve," I continued in laying out the theme.

"Well, no, Erin. I wouldn't say that. She knew I was trying to do better, and I could only do that by leaving. She supported me. She didn't like it, but she understood," Mom shared.

"Ok, well, I remember you saying we stopped going to church because you felt like an outcast for being divorced."

"Well, she didn't know that! She thought we were going to church!" Mom roared.

"Oh, come on, Mom. She knew. I was the only one of her 25 grandchildren to not go through first communion and be confirmed. She knew. She may have turned a blind eye, but she knew."

"Well, you got confirmed," as if that negated her non-church going.

"Mom! I got confirmed after she died!" I laughed.

"Well, she knew that, too!"

My Mom asked me to read her passages from what I had written years ago. She giggled through my description of the lush lawns of UVA. She loved what she heard.

"I don't know where you get all those words and ideas from... I could never have that much to say," she said as a compliment.

She said she loved the book topic and had never thought about the connections between her story, my grandmothers and great grandmothers and mine. She said she was truly blown away thinking about it out loud.

She first asked how I plan to tie the stories together. "What do these four women have to do with each other?"

"It's a story about the pursuit of love and happiness in lives across generations, in this imperfect struggle called life, we pursued love and happiness,"

I gave examples from her to my Grandmother, as I saw her. "My story is connected to hers. Your story is connected to hers. We are connected across generations in the same ways and we all have in common imperfection but deep pursuit of love and happiness despite that."

"Erin, it was. It really was the pursuit of happiness. I wanted better for you girls and a better job was the only way to get there and not be poor any more. I was tired of being poor. And I had to get out of Tampa," she said, offering details to me for one of the first times about her life's difficult choices.

She was tired of being poor. So, she moved her kids to a better life.

She gave me her blessing. Now, I felt free to call Marbury and ask him to meet with me.

--
November 2 – Tapping Uncle Marbury

"Ohhhh, her story isn't as bleak as she told it," he chortled right off saying to me during our first phone call.

"Martyrdom. *'Ohhh. Lay it on me'*," he said, mocking her voice.

After about 20 minutes of mostly listening, I had just told him the reason I wanted to visit was I wanted to talk about Granny's story and the Zimmers.

Marbury recounted his own conversations with his mother, Dorothy. I knew instantly this was going to be good.

"Mother said *'oh my Father abused my poor Mother!'*"

"How do you figure?' I'd say to her…"

"She said 'Oh he took advantage of her and got her pregnant ...with ME!'" he said, shouting as if he was Dorothy feeling pain with the words.

"And I'd say 'and you don't think he had any help?'"

"'Excuse me! He didn't have any help,' Dot said"

"Who the hell do you think helped your mother get out of all those damn clothes? A brassiere, a corset? A slip? Before you even got the dress off, you had to take that thing off – that thing that was sticking out about a foot from her ass."

What you can't do is hear those words the way he pronounced them in his special Southern Maryland accent. What he said was "*Aboot a fut from her ayss*". I loved the familiarity of that accent, as it is my Mother's, too, and not the same one I hear in the Deep South.

Marbury continued with the history lesson, "Early 1900's women, socially-prominent, wealthy people wore the things under their dress that caused the back of the dress to stick out. Purpose of the device was to cover their asses."

"The lengths they went to just to use the bathroom. Just to tinkle. They just stepped into the bushes and did their duty. No toilet paper. No underwear. Just take a squat."

And just like that, his blessing was delivered.

"I'd like to come to your house next Thursday, if that's okay with you. Will you be home?" I asked.

I had never in my adult life proposed a visit to my Uncle Marbury.

"Well, yes. What time are you thinking?" he said.

"What time do you wake up? How about 10am?" I asked. I was not sure how to ask for a visit from out of state and tried to not sound like I was scheduling a business appointment, but I couldn't help how eager I was. I wanted to confirm this thing.

"That's fine," Marbury said, as if we were done.

"Do you want to know what I want to know – my questions?" I asked, feeling there was more I needed to explain before venturing 800 miles.

"You can write them down and drop them in the mail," he said.

"You don't want me to email them instead?" I asked, thinking the timeline of 6 days was too tight for me to physically mail anything.

"I don't fuss with that anymore. Just mail them if you want."

"Okay, I will," I assured him.

I was headed North to uncover this landmine with Marbury. I couldn't believe it.

I promptly hand wrote him a letter including my main questions out on legal yellow paper.

Dear Marbury,
I look forward to seeing you and Gloria. In case it is helpful, I thought I'd send a few topics/questions I'm interested in. Of course, I'll hear whatever you wish to share beyond this, but this will give you a clue as to what I am thinking about.
1) *What was the catalyst for Dorothy seeking out the Zimmers? Did it happen quickly, or over several months/years?*
2) *Did she ever actually meet William, her brother? Did her sister Polly know about Granny's existence, or just William? Polly eventually settled in Louisville, Kentucky, and had her own line of Mary Blair's. Did Granny know about them?*
3) *I've heard Sam walked in front of a car to intentionally kill himself. I've heard Polly died young from overdose. What is actually true?*
4) *I've heard about your visit to William in 1962. How did he treat you? Was he an ass? Was he kind? What was your goal?*

5) Was it known to Granny that my mom used the false name of "Anna Zimmer" that time in 1962-63? How did she feel about it?
6) What else am I missing?

I'll see you Thursday. Call if you need anything.

Love you,
Erin
Ps. Hi, Gloria. ☺

One week after introducing my mother to the book idea and winning her blessing, I took off to Maryland to visit with my uncle Marbury, her brother.

"Be safe. Take a picture with my brother and Gloria," her text read.

"So many questions to get answered!" I replied excitedly, as I headed to the airport.

--
Day 9 – at Marbury's home in Indian Head, Maryland – November 8

Marbury's telling of the tale was like looking at a treasure map, complete with detours, treasure troves, and landmines.

This day in November, I had travelled 700-plus miles to Indian Head, Maryland, where I met with my uncle Marbury in the living room of his house on Beecher Avenue. As I stepped up to his house for the first time in 20 years, his red brick home was incredibly familiar to my much-younger memory.

My visit arrived with the peak of Fall foliage, with the Dogwoods gleaming bright reds and purples in what felt like a warm triumphant welcome to the release of these old, silent secrets. The air was chilly, and I wondered if this was the same chilly air that Polly felt when she discovered she was pregnant with Sam's baby yet still unmarried – at this very same time of year just a few counties away.

The smell of fall was in the air. The soil was wet. The air was crisp. My conscience was clear.

Marbury and I talked on day one for about 11 hours in his living room. We talked a lot, we ate lunch and then dinner. We moved not more than one inch from our respective cozy chairs, except for necessary trips to the bathroom. We took occasional breaks to provide color commentary on Judge Judy's handing out of justice to a parade of low-lifes.

Marbury did most of the talking, ranging on topics from the French revolution, the Louisiana purchase, illegitimate children of kings, the black folks in Charles County, my grandmother's pursuit of her birthright, my mother's choice, my father's Peter Pan syndrome, Sam's lifetime of lies, and his own teenage adventures to bring together his mother and William Zimmer.

Gloria made us turkey sandwiches for lunch, and never let my glass of Iced Tea stay empty for long. Before I knew it, she had also cooked dinner, serving me up a plate of delicious white meat chicken, baked potato (already buttered and salted and peppered), broccoli, and a buttered biscuit.

Then before I knew it, I had dessert sitting in front of me as well, which was a baked Winchester apple from Aunt Jo's with a dollop of ice cream on top. Gloria's cooking made me feel right at home. I quickly wished I had just planned to stay with them longer.

I was transported to another time and space there in Marbury's living room. It was as if the doors of history had been flung open, and he was eager to tell the story. For the first time in his life, someone was as passionate about his Mother's truth as he was.

I learned that Sam may have walked in front of a car on purpose, most likely because he knew the baby he'd abandoned was now an adult woman who was coming to find him and expose his lifetime of lies. Sam's lies were the same frauds that not only orphaned Dorothy, but likely underwrote Polly's untimely, young death.

"Mother and Daddy married in 1937 when she was 28 and Daddy was 30. Elizabeth born in '38. Mary Blair in '40, Trish in '42, Jo in '44. She got out of high school at 16 from St. Mary's Academy, she'd been bumped ahead a grade," Marbury ran through *that* set of facts quickly.

Marbury was only 16 when he visited William. He was still in high school boarding in Washington, D.C. when he hopped on a train in Union Station headed to Richmond. He'd told his family he was staying in D.C. to go to a dance at St. Anthony's. He certainly didn't tell them he was going down to visit his mother's long-lost brother, William Zimmer, III.

"I knew where he was because his address was in the Richmond directory. I went to his work; he was expecting me. I told him I was coming. I just called him from a payphone."

"He knew as soon as I walked in who I was."

"I spent the night in Richmond."

"He had that narrow face that the Walker family had. He wasn't a very good-looking man as far as I was concerned. I sure wasn't interested in him!"

"He said he didn't believe Mother was his mother and father's daughter, 'she may be my father's, but not my mother's, she wouldn't have done *that.*'"

"When I think about Sam, and I think about Polly. Polly was a gorgeous woman."

"What in the hell did Polly ever see in the man she married, I'll never know. He was one of these men who prowled from one bed to the next."

--
A Journey to Forgiveness

Knowingly or not, Marbury had come to own the same disdain for Sam that his mother Dorothy owned her whole life. As much as he critiqued his mother's unwillingness to contact the Zimmers, he shared her scornful narrative of Sam-the-philanderer.

"Polly when she died, she probably took an overdose. Not accidentally, but deliberately because Sam was going around with this other woman. He waited a year and then married her right after Polly died."

"Respectability. That's what these people were all about." Marbury scoffed.

Was it *all* they were about? Or was it a *myth* of the Zimmers that covered deep wounds?

Marbury and his Mother had a thorny relationship to all observers, but he was fiercely loyal to her. In profound fidelity to their bond, her psychic antagonists became his own. He hated the myth of Sam with every bit of passion that his Mother did. In many ways, however, this passion was a testament to the devotion his Mother cultivated with her children.

Deserving hate or not, Sam did what he had to do to live up to the expectations, family obligations, and ambitions placed upon him. Sam's surviving family members, William, Jr. and Puggy were wrestling with the aftermath of Sam's shocking death when Dorothy appeared in 1931 out of nowhere to claim her birthright. Not only had their brother died a shocking death, but they were left to claim the mantle and raise his teenage children.

Did they reject her out of *respectability*?

Or were they trying to save young Polly and Billy from further tumult, as they'd already lost both parents in the span of three years. Gaining a new sister out of thin air may have simply been impossible for grieving teens to comprehend. In any case, it was incomprehensible for William, Jr., and Puggy.

Their rejection pained Dorothy in real ways and suspended her ability to gain closure on her birth story.

Aggrieved by the Zimmers now double-rejection at birth and again in 1931, Dorothy nonetheless gained much from this rejection.

She gained two parents in Bertha and George who loved her and doted upon her. Bertha mothered her with mental stability and diligence. She gave Dorothy education and as much opportunity to grow as she could from Indian Head, Maryland. To have been orphaned, yet land so well – Dorothy's luck was ironically good.

Marbury shared his Mother's strength, even as it clashed with hers. It was no surprise, then, to watch him interminably guard Dorothy's dignity during and beyond her lifetime. In listening to him tell her story to me, I observed the essence of what her pain created.

Resilience.

Stubborn values.

Strength.

Loyalty.

These stand tall as the pillars of Dorothy Bryan's legacy. As if by osmosis, her seven children would also absorb these into the structures of their lives. Indeed, even as her grandchild, in the greatest trials of my life I have called upon HER strength and dignity to embolden me.

Little did I know the depth of her story then as I do now. Sure, I knew her to be mighty, and I revered her. Yet, my reverence could not see past her strength to understand what purpose it served for her.

I could not see strength was her shield. The landmines we thought were ours were actually hers – and were not even landmines for her, but ever-tender, deeply-protected wounds.

Dorothy was a young, ambitious and industrious woman whose adult life crashed into – and *was always inextricable from* – her birth story. Destiny simply revealed the stark truths surrounding her birth that many of us are spared.

Yet her story reveals a common, shared struggle for happiness that humans endlessly seek.

Dorothy would have been a toddler, settling into Mother B's home late in 1911, the same year Sara Pryor published her last book, *The Colonel's Story*. In Sara's culminating work, she introduced a compassionate character named Mrs. Bangs. Mrs. Bangs was blessed with a tendency to touch "sorrow too sacred for discussion."

In a soothing reflection on life's tragedies, Mrs. Bangs says solemnly:

> "We sholy does walk in a vale o' tears. This worl's
> a wil'erness o' woe as the hime says."

Sara, through Mrs. Bangs' voice, wrote this prose as poetry. In Sara's fictional world, Mrs. Bangs was the truth-teller, the feelings-knower. There was healing possible through her words, even when others felt too sorrowful to speak of their own woe.

For sure, "early" babies, Victorian edicts aimed at eschewing illegitimacy and impropriety created a *wilderness of woe* and toxic secrets for many. Yet, in unveiling the truth, we allow ourselves to more freely pursue happiness, free from the most toxic of social constraints, and free to construct our individuality.

In a wilderness of *truth*, we will experience woe, yet we are free to develop deep bonds and fidelity with others. Fidelity in our bonds allow us to be vulnerable – and to heal. Secret sorrows too sacred for discussion can be healed when we reveal our deepest truths and vulnerabilities.

Truth produces fidelity.

Truth and fidelity in pain permit sorrow that can be shared.

Sorrow allows for healing.

Healing earns us freedom.

When we gain freedom from woe we have endured, we embolden others to endure life's moments of tragedy, supported by our forged bonds of love.

Truth brings love.

Dorothy's sorrow was too sacred for conversation.

Still, in absolutely brave and independent determination, she unveiled truths of her secret birth. Though painful, the truth released her to pursue her own life built upon her own merits and defined by her own fidelities. Her Catholicism, her family, and her thoroughness to every detail defined and structured her being. The truth pushed her toward her destiny.

Dorothy's truth created the present moment. A moment where her 18th grandchild can write freely of our liberation from secrets, shame, and lies.

Her wilderness of woe is one which created so many lives; inspired strength in developing girls and fear in recalcitrant boys.

Her woe gave birth to a large, bonded family – this family – born in rejection yet raised in the pursuit of love.

June's sunsets will blaze evermore in full, unabashed, unashamed glory to Dorothy's resilience and brilliance. Her path was unexpected, and would have broken weaker women, but she persisted and pursued love. Her destiny's landscape was captured best in her own words to all of us in 1989 following her triumphant 80th birthday celebration:

"Venisti, Vidisti, Vicisti!"

Dorothy came, she saw, she conquered, indeed.

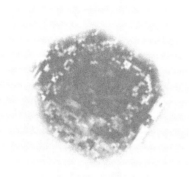

ERIN L. RICHMAN

22

Epilogue

The Split Tree: What if each branch knew the other?

What if the sisters-Mary Blair would have known each other later in life, after their families were formed? What if Polly looked into the eyes of her older sister, Dorothy, and saw the same beautiful, bouncy, full head of wavy hair? And the same attention to every detail of clothing and accessories? And the saw the same short stature, even for a woman?

The two sisters were born 13 months apart and died six months apart. They shared space on this Earth for 86 years and nine months. Though what would have happened if they knew each other?

What might our family become when or if we meet relatives from the other branch? And what becomes of 'family' as we know it? We were lost tribes, lost from each other.

How would Dorothy's children react to meeting their first cousins – their beloved Mother's siblings' flesh and blood? The only cousins they would have ever known in their lives? They had only ever known each other. For all magnificent seven of them, family equaled siblings, no cousins –ever.

They assumed their whole lives that they were inferior, and truly among the unwanted. How will their worlds turn if they are embraced – in place of their mother – at this stage of life? What would Dorothy think?

After taking a journey deep into my grandmother's life, I had even more questions. However, I was unsure how to get answers, or *if* I could even get them. No one had ever tried reaching out. Did they know our side existed and they rejected us knowingly? Did they have no clue? Perhaps it was finally time to close the broken loop.

I truly thought I would never get answers. I could not at least try without asking.

Did that half of the family tree even know the tree had been split 100 years ago, and that there is another fully thriving branch?

I spent about eight years pondering, writing drafts of letters, and trying to decipher what the best thing to do was. Each time, I decided I was crazy to reopen this up. Each time, I let it go.

"I would ask myself, "Why in the world would I want to reach out to these people? Why do I want this?"

I never had an answer for myself. I had enough family, I told myself, and I knew it to be true. There was no good reason to make contact, at least not one that outweighed the risk.

"They will think I am crazy, or worse, they will be mean," I would tell myself, convincing myself each time to not reach out.

What if *they* – in present day – became yet another landmine? Or, better yet, what if they did *not*?

Every couple of years, this 'split branch' of family crept back into my mind. And I retraced my steps of researching. Seeing names and faces of not-so-distant relatives up on Google, Facebook, and old newspapers renewed my curiosity every time it snuck back in my mind.

I finally decided to write a letter to my Granny's lost tribe. I wrote as though I would want to be written to. I figured if my best effort in a letter appealed to them, then probably they shared something in common with me. If not, no loss was incurred and all would be well.

I went to the Hallmark store, inspected their special stationery, and carefully selected the thickest paper with a classic blue border. I typed the message on my computer, and in it, I emphasized my desire to respect boundaries.

When I wrote the letter, my main goal was to NOT sound crazy. I wanted to come across as a rational, intelligent person (which I think I am). And, perhaps, if I was really lucky, I might have a chance to talk and ask some basic questions, fill some holes in.

Dr. Erin L. Richman

November 30, 2018

Ms. Lee ▮▮▮▮
▮▮▮▮▮▮▮▮
Louisville, KY ▮▮▮

Dear Ms. ▮▮▮▮:

I am writing to you with cheer and good will as your first-cousin-once-removed whom you've never met. Please allow me to explain.

My name is Dr. Erin Richman, 45, and I reside in Jacksonville Beach, Florida, where I serve as an Associate Vice President at a local college here in Florida. For the past 8-9 years, one enduring interest of mine has been conducting research into my grandmother's remarkable life. I've known virtually my entire life that my grandmother was adopted, born in Washington DC as the biological child of **Samuel & "Polly"** (Mary Blair Walker) **Zimmer**. My grandmother's birth certificate reflects this; however, she was raised to adulthood by another couple in southern Maryland.

I have learned the circumstances of Polly's 1909 pregnancy and my grandmother's resulting birth in June 1909 through extensive research. The story is stranger than fiction, though understandably the result of a very different era in American history.

Clearly you and I have not met, but I am reaching out to simply introduce myself and offer you peace in honor of Polly Walker Zimmer and also in honor of my grandmother. Polly never had the pleasure of knowing my grandmother, her first born daughter, as Sam quickly returned them back to Petersburg after her birth and never saw her again, leaving her in the delivery doctor's care in DC. Were she alive today, my grandmother would probably not condone my writing to you, out of respect for privacy and her own self-respect. She was a dignified and remarkable woman. So, I sincerely apologize now on her behalf if you find this is an unwelcome gesture.

I adored my grandmother and share her likeness, along with my mother's. She provided us with a deep and enduring example of being a "Mother," and profound desire to live up to her maternal legacy of strength, love, and resilience.

Though my grandmother passed in 1997 at 88, she lived a long, fruitful life. She discovered accidently at age 21 her birth story, which took its fateful turn when Sam Zimmer, your maternal grandfather, decided to give her away because she had been conceived prior to his and Polly's marriage. She moved on, had 7 children of her own and 24 grandchildren, of which I am 15th. Her 6 daughters and one son are alive and now in their 70's. We grandchildren span our 30-50's.

I am also aware that Polly and Sam had three more children: your mother, Mary Blair "Polly" Zimmer *Cochran* (1910); William Louis Zimmer (1912), and an infant son Samuel (1916), buried with Polly in Petersburg. William (your uncle) corresponded by letter with my grandmother many times over the course of their adulthoods, though they never met in person. I'm unclear to what extent your mother Polly ever knew of my grandmother's existence, though my grandmother certainly knew of her brother and sister's existence.

Assuming my research is correct, then, you are my grandmother Dorothy's niece (as her younger sister Polly's daughter), and you are also my mother Anna's first cousin. I've enclosed a few photos so you can put faces together with these names.

Let me draw this note to a close by acknowledging this letter may be a surprise to receive, and - quite possibly - unbelievable. I can only imagine how I would react if I were you. You may even be wondering why, after a century and a generation has passed, I would be writing with this old news. I know - it may seem bizarre.
Since learning the outlines of her family origin, I have been deeply curious to simply know whether you have ever been aware of her existence (or not)? And, either way, would you possibly be interested in meeting? I would like to ask a few questions to help me understand a few aspects of Polly's and William's life. *I deeply respect your right to privacy regardless of whether we meet once in the future or not.*

Perhaps, one day might we meet over coffee to learn more about what Polly Walker Zimmer's separated surviving children created for this world? Thank you for reading and best wishes.

Most sincerely,

Erin Richman

Dorothy visiting 244 Sycamore St. in Petersburg in 1985.

My grandmother, Dorothy Bryan (1909-1997, aka Mary Blair Zimmer).

My mother, Anna Bryan Richman.

I wanted to be personal, but professional. Well-written and polished, but humanized. I enclosed pictures of my mother and my grandmother, including one of my Granny posed on the steps of the Zimmer family home at 244 S. Sycamore Street in Petersburg. I was unsure if these were nice or mean people. I was unsure of everything.

The three letters were virtually identical, except for changing of pronouns and addressees. I told very brief outlines of the family connection, and how Sam and Polly left the baby, my grandmother, in D.C. to eventually be raised by another couple. I expressed my deep reverence for my grandmother, and a desire to honor her legacy by reaching out. My intention was not to invade privacy or disrupt. I wanted to close a loop that had been broken, in honor of my remarkable, resilient grandmother.

I signed and sent my letter. I crafted it with careful attention to how it would be handled and viewed by its receiver. I expected nothing, and if something more than nothing happened, I could not envision what it would be. All I knew is that I had to at least *try* communicating with them.

Did they have any clue at all that my grandmother existed?

What was Polly's and William's life like after their mother died?

What do they know about grandmother Polly's death? *[what death certificate says]*

What do they know about Sam Zimmer's death?

Did your mother ever talk about Polly, her mother? What was your mother's memory of her mother? Happy/sad? Did they know? Why did she do it? Was there ever suspicion of Sam?

In our family, the lore has been that Sam purposefully walked in front of a car. Did they share that perception? Or did they think he just had bad luck?

At a minimum, my letter would let the other side of our split family tree that we, in fact, exist and have rather strong branches of our own. In the best-case scenario, I would actually meet with them once or so to learn more about the Zimmer family and fix what broke so long ago.

If my hunch was right, each recipient was my mother's first cousin, and my Granny's niece or nephew, who likely had zero idea she even ever existed. I sent the first to a Zimmer cousin in Palm Beach via FedEx, and got confirmation of its delivery the next day. A week went by, still no call or email. There was no reply at all.

The only person who knew that I had sent this letter was my sister, Sharon. She would text me every day and ask, "hear anything yet?" I kept her updated on the no-response. I did not tell my mother.

After a week went by, Sharon pushed me to send the exact same letter to the other cousins in Louisville and Richmond using the exact same stationery. It had not occurred to me to do that, so I did. I sent the second batch out exactly one week after sending the first.

Finally, a week later, I received a phone call during a work meeting from a strange number in Louisville, KY. I sent it to voicemail, as I could not answer it right then in the middle of this meeting in a small room around a conference table with my brand-new boss. I wondered if this caller could possibly be the same person in KY to whom I'd mailed one of the letters. "Nah," I told myself and put my phone down.

I put my focus back on the meeting topic and tuned back into the voices of the people sitting in the room with me. I was physically present, but the voice in my head kept thinking, "Louisville!? What are the odds?"

I was soon dying to check the voicemail. There was no way in the meeting to listen to it, I reasoned with myself. I continued to try to focus on the meeting occurring in front of me.

With the suspense killing me and unable to think about anything else, I picked up my phone during the meeting and navigating over to the missed calls and voicemails. I peeked at the text transcription on my iPhone. I saw the name "Lee" and the city name "Louisville Kentucky" in the text transcription. My eyes must have bugged three inches out of my head. My heart rate skyrocketed and I got lightheaded. My lips were tingling and my hands got cold.

I immediately stopped myself from reading the transcription. I did not want to read anything disappointing or rejecting during a work meeting, just in case her tone was mean. If her tone was nice, I wanted to be fully present and savor it in honor of my grandmother. I didn't want to miss a thing.

I wanted to be physically alone and mentally prepared for whatever her voicemail might say. My brain was on fire with thoughts of "oh my God, she really called!" and "what the hell do I do now!?" and "oh my God, am I really ready for this!?"

An hour later, I got in my car – alone – to drive to lunch and kept my phone in my hand as I slid down into the driver's seat. I sat for a moment. I took a deep breath. I stared at the speedometer as my car remained turned off.

When I was calm enough to listen, I realized she would likely not have called if she was going to be unfriendly. An unfriendly person does not leave a long message, and even glancing at the transcription without reading I could tell it was lengthy. My gut told me this was going to be a friendly message. And I began to cry tears for my grandmother. Perhaps this long-awaited moment had come, and all in one moment I felt relief, terror, sorrow, grief, and joy. Tears rolled down my face, releasing decades of shame.

I collected myself and I listened to the voicemail.

Her voice came through as clear, warm, booming, and affectionate. Old school southern with butter and sugar on top.

"*Dr. Richman, it's Lee ▇▇▇ in Louisville, Kentucky. My!! [laughter] What a start to the holiday season! Uh, powerful letter. Extraordinary information. I am more than glad that you reached out. I just literally opened your letter and, uh, I look forward to, if it's alright with you, contacting you after we get through the holidays, chatting, and seeing who and how we can know more about one another and share whatever it is that makes sense to share for us to share. Uh, I am very grateful for you having reached out, If you want to give me a call or just wait til after Christmas, either one will work for me. I look forward to, uh, speaking with you in the not too distant future. Best wishes for our family[laughter], our WHOLE family, for the holiday season and new year. Thank you again, Bye bye."*

"Glad." "Very Grateful." "Thank you again."

Did she really just say "thank you?"

"Powerful." "Extraordinary." Ok, she liked the letter and I didn't seem crazy.

"Our family... our whole family."

What? Did she just call us "family?" Are we family? I guess we are family. Yes, we are family. Wow.

"I look forward to talking to you in the not-too-distant future."

She wants to talk. Oh my god.

She really spoke those words. She really sounded warm, sincere, and even loving in her voicemail to me. WOW.

She was just pure WOW. I felt pure WOW. Blown away does not describe it fully.

Breaking through the sound barrier, entering another dimension might describe the feeling I had. It felt as though I pierced the barrier for my grandmother. The broken loop was closing.

She couldn't believe there was this branch unknown. I could not believe she called. I never went to lunch that day. I just sat alone in my car with my tears and my gratitude, deeply hoping my grandmother could feel what I felt, wherever her spirit was in the universe.

'Lee, you need to start over again'

Two days later after I received the voicemail from Lee, I had the rare opportunity to be alone without interruption to do some writing. It was a Saturday morning and Sara and the girls were gone doing some holiday festivities. I elected to cash in on birthday week by having time to write.

It was December 8, 2018: 110 years after Sam and Polly likely discovered they were pregnant with my grandmother.

When my phone rang, I saw her name come up and I paused my jazz music, and I cleared my throat for God knows what.

My eyes widened and I sat up.

Here, at this moment, over a century later, was the meeting of Sam and Polly's split tree. Their children's children would connect. Their 20th century secret shame would be accepted openly and warmly in the 21st century.

"Helloooo?" I answered with a welcoming lilt, knowing already who was on the other end, but still hesitant of what was to come.

"Erin?" the voice asked.

"Yes, hi," I replied excitedly.

"This is Lee ▮▮▮▮▮▮," she said and let out an exhorted chuckle.

Returning the enthusiasm, I blurted, "Well, good morning!"

And then a second of silence and nervous chuckles.

I filled in the silence, saying, "If I can say this first, I have no idea what to say. I did not prepare for this moment!"

"Neither do I," she laughed again.

"When I wrote that letter, my main goal was to not sound crazy. I didn't want to scare anyone. Those were my minimum hopes. At best, I hoped I might actually get a chance to talk to you. Which is what we are doing right now, and, honestly, I did not think this would happen so I have NO IDEA what to say other than, hi and thank you."

She laughed throughout what I said. Her warmth and humanity put me at ease. Admitting to my bland introduction set the expectation at precisely zero.

I instantly felt like *"THIS is someone I will enjoy talking to."*

She started right off, saying, *"I have to tell you, when I first started reading the letter, I thought this was one of those, 'I'm your cousin in Africa starting a cleft palate charity...'* I cackled and she continued. "Then I saw the name Zimmer...and thought whoa... so I paused and thought "You need to start over again.'

"I started over and started counting down generations."

"I called my cousin in Palm Beach. And she said she got a letter, too, a few weeks ago."

"My cousin said to me, 'I don't know what to do with it. I don't have time to deal with this right now.'

"Well, I, on the other hand, picked up the phone right away. I had a friend who had an aunt show up out of nowhere. So, I guess it is our turn," she chuckled.

"My sister, Polly is here in Louisville, Polly is frail. We decided not to tell her right away. It is better she not know just yet."

"We will tell her children. So, they may override us. And that's their choice."

"Really, I don't know how much you will hear from the other side," she explained, as if to help me not be disappointed.

"My cousin's reaction was very different from mine. She's got a deep southern accent [impersonating her], 'I don't know what to do with it!'" Lee said with a beautifully-imitated and exquisite Virginia drawl.

"We are midwestern, pragmatic. They are old school, Virginian. My daughter has been calling me every day, 'have you talked to her?! Have you talked to her?' Just a different reaction here on our end. And that's ok."

We proceeded to exchange questions and answers.

Did you know about us? *Not a clue.*

"Who raised Polly and William after their parents died?" I asked. *"Puggy (Aunt Margaret) and Uncle Billy at 244 S. Sycamore Street. We traveled there every Christmas and they were the only grandparents I ever knew,"* Lee recounted.

"How did your grandmother come to visit 244 S. Sycamore?" Lee asked, curiously.

"She actually made trips to Petersburg once or twice a year and did drive-bys," I shared. I told her the story of Marbury in the car, Marbury peering over the fence and being invited in for lemonade in 1962.

I told Lee the story of Marbury visiting William at A.H. Robins. I told how William and Dot exchanged letters. I explained that I assumed you all knew we existed since William knew of her.

"The picture I sent you was taken in 1986 when she and her daughter/ my aunt Mary Blair, visited, and the Episcopal Diocese let her in. My mother and her siblings also even visited several years ago, and the doctor who owns it let them in and showed them around. There was always this wonderment from afar. It was in the oxygen in the air in the family, but she very clearly prohibited her children from contacting the

Zimmers. Whether it was out of respect for them, or maybe self-protective, or both, it was understood," I spoke with somber tone.

"Did your grandmother have a family with the parents who raised her?" Lee asked.

"Yes, but very small, no cousins. She created a large family for herself," I chuckled.

What was mother-Polly like? *Polly was a very beautiful woman, as was my mother. But Polly had severe migraines. She suffered from them, as did my mother and my sister. She died when my mother was a teenager, so Puggy stepped in. Puggy was the matriarch.*

The questions continued like ping-pong balls back and forth.

"Do you see any resemblance in the pictures I shared?" I asked.

"Not so much in Dorothy, but definitely in your Mother. Your Mother really favors. Polly and my mother were beautiful, as is your Mother, with those eyes. And my cousin has that look as well," Lee offered.

"How did Dorothy discover she was adopted?" Lee asked, as any reasonable person would.

I told the story of Dorothy applying for a typist-clerk job in 1931, when she worked at the Census. She needed her birth certificate. That was the catalyst, and led to the unfolding of the story to her, I recounted in detail.

"I am just so sorry for the pain Dorothy must have felt," she said, as if I could literally see the heft of her sorrow through the phone. It was as if my grandmother's sorrow was collapsing in present-time, with Lee's sincere and authentic empathy releasing it for good. It is amazing how one person's empathy can heal another's pain.

I said, "Well, I look at it this way, if anything had been different – if Sam had not given her up, if she'd been part of the Zimmer world, I wouldn't exist... none of her children would exist, none of my cousins would exist. As difficult as it may have been for her, this was our fate, it is what it is, and she created a family that fulfilled her. She lived a very good life." And that is how I saw it, I explained.

"Do you have any plans for Christmas?" Lee asked, shifting to lighter topics.

"Yes, we are hosting my mother and my sisters' families at my house this year, so that will be fun," I shared, hoping to convey again that I am not a lonely serial killer looking to adopt a family.

"Good," she said in approval.

"How about you?" I asked of her in return.

"Well, I have a daughter and a son. She hasn't found Mr. Right. My daughter has two kids from in vitro. So, she has twins. Thankful she didn't have 6 or 7 kids! My son is here also. I get them together for Christmas at my house, whether they like it or not," Lee said with such great humor and energy.

I did not say it, but the thought flashed in my head –"How funny, ironic. I have two kids from an anonymous donor, too. Just one hundred years earlier, Sam and Polly abandoned my grandmother because she was merely conceived out of wedlock even though she was born in wedlock. Now, two of Sam and Polly's great-granddaughters have our beautiful children from men we have never even met. We truly have come full circle!

We continued chatting with pleasantries, before I soon asked, "Who is Polly Cunningham?"

"Yes, she is my niece. Polly Blakemore Cunningham. And Neville Blakemore is my nephew, her brother. They are my sister Polly's children. They are named Mary Blair as well," Lee explained to me.

I respond, "A Polly Cunningham came up on 23&me as a second cousin. The name "Polly" made me think she might be part of your side's line of Mary Blairs."

I continued, "We have our own line of Mary Blairs! I guess once my grandmother had her children, and knew her birthright, she claimed it for herself and named her daughter Mary Blair, as a way to claim her place amongst Mary Blair's. We called them Mary Blair, though, not Polly. How unique is that – to have a name Mary Blair?

"Yes!" Lee replied, "It really is!"

The Mary Blair link was now unbroken. All that was left was to fill everyone in on the branches and see how they would choose to connect.

Lee and I, we completed the first, most delayed step. It was an amazing, healing thing for wounds I myself did not know were mine yet which lived on in my grandmother's children, collectively, unconsciously.

In just one conversation, our split branches connected. I felt touched by her healing words and voice.

The landmines of rejection and exclusion were exposed, no longer shrouded in secrecy and propriety. Dorothy's sorrow – a sorrow too sacred for discussion – was privately carried for most of her years, yet released in the tears shared between Lee and me.

Lee and I both cried for Dorothy. Lee cried upon realizing Dorothy's unimaginable pain of rejection, her burdens carried while driving past South Sycamore all those years, literally an outsider to the family inside the iron gates. I cried in catharsis – joy mixed with relief and disbelief.

Dorothy's honor and worth were a settled matter.

A century-old landmine was definitively disarmed, now incapable of haunting any further.

Finally, in that present moment, the quiet acknowledgement and sincere apology salved Dorothy's grief. I accepted the salve on her behalf – *gladly*.

She was secret no longer, with the past a closed book except for the good times…

23 Appendix
Of *Dorothy's* Destiny

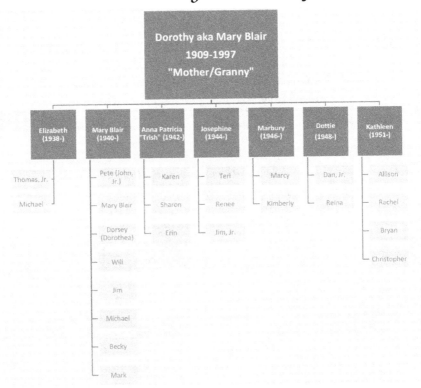

Dorothy's Branch of the Mary Blair Tree:
- Born as "Mary Blair" to Samuel Zimmer & Mary Blair Polly Walker Zimmer, of Petersburg, married Jan 1909
- Birthed in June, 1909, in Washington DC in rented room of boarding house; fostered by midwife until age 2
- Never legally adopted, but raised by Bertha & George Hardy in Indian Head, MD; went to private Catholic boarding school
- Resided from ages 2-85 (1911-95) in Indian Head, MD, where she worked on US Navy base, raised children
- Resided 1995-1997 in Tampa, FL., where she died; buried in Indian Head, MD
- Both of her given names appear on gravestone marker: "Dorothy Hardy Bryan born Mary Blair Zimmer"
- **Dorothy** had **7** children, **24** grandchildren, **47** great-grandchildren, **10** great-great grandchildren

Elizabeth Bryan Milstead, **80**, lives on the Chicamuxen River in Indian Head, MD.
Mary Blair Bryan Peterson, **78**, lives in Spring Hill, FL.
Anna "**Trish**" Bryan Richman, **76**, lives in Jacksonville Beach, FL.
Josephine Bryan Reklis, **74**, lives in Winchester, VA.
Alexander **Marbury** Bryan, **72**, lives in Indian Head, MD.
Dorothy **Dottie** Bryan Garcia, **70**, lives in Green Valley, AZ.
Kathleen Bryan Peterson, **67**, lives in Riverview, FL.

24

Complete List of Children, Grandchildren, Great-grandchildren, & Great-great Grandchildren of Dorothy Stuart Hardy Bryan, 1909-1997, nèe Mary Blair Pryor Walker Zimmer

Children (7)

Elizabeth Ellen Bryan Milstead
Mary Blair Bryan Peterson
Anna Patricia Bryan Richman
Josephine Clagett Bryan Reklis
Alexander Marbury Bryan, III
Dorothy Regina Bryan Garcia
Kathleen Theresa Bryan Peterson

Grandchildren (24)

John Peterson, Jr.	Renèe Baratka (Koski)
Mary Blair Peterson (Mirabal)	Daniel Garcia, Jr.
	Sharon Richman (Porter)
Thomas Milstead, Jr.	Mark Peterson
Theresa Baratka (Howell)	Marcy Bryan (Gannon)
Dorothea Peterson (Fiorello)	James Baratka, Jr.
William Peterson	Erin L. Richman
Michael Milstead	Allison Peterson (Macri)
James Peterson	Kimberly Bryan
Michael Peterson	Reina-Marie Garcia (Balach)
Rebecca Peterson (Weintraub)	Rachel Peterson (Chunn)
Karen Richman (Bailey/Haynes)	Bryan Peterson
	Christopher Peterson

OF MARY BLAIR DESTINY

Great-Grandchildren (48)

Kristina Peterson	Chris Weintraub	Alexandra Richman
Blair Marie Mirabal	Chelsea Bailey	Cassandra Richman
Dino Mirabal, Jr.	Catherine Bailey	Isabella Macri
Paul Fiorello	Jordy Bailey	Chase Macri
Sean Milstead	Cameron Haynes	Aleksandar Balach
Paige Milstead	Haylie Koski	Lukas Chunn
Bryan Howell	Thomas Koski	Hannah Chunn
Lee Howell	Jason Porter	Logan Chunn
Jessie Milstead	Mason Porter	Elise Peterson
Nicole Milstead	Andrew Porter	Lili Blair Peterson
James Peterson, Jr.	Alexa Gannon	
Virginia Peterson	Marissa Gannon	
John F. Peterson	Megan Blair	
Lauren Peterson	Peterson	
Alexander Peterson	Zachary Peterson	
Matthew Peterson	Adam Garcia	
Annie Peterson	Michael Garcia	
Maggie Peterson	Joseph Baratka	
Sophie Peterson	Jordan Baratka	

Great-Great-Grandchildren (11)

Caiden Peterson	Isabella Bailey
Bella Marie Dean	Raiden Peterson
Nathan Dean	Poppy Lee Peterson
Camden Mirabal	James Peterson, III
Taylor Mirabal	Emmie Peterson
Lily Howell	

ERIN L. RICHMAN

Alexander Marbury and Dorothy Hardy Bryan, 1944

L-R: Marbury, IV, Trish, Mary Blair, Dottie, Liz, Josephine.
Not pictured, Kathleen.

L-R: Marbury IV, Dorothy with Kathleen, Mary Blair, Trish,
Josephine, Marbury III, Dottie, Liz.

Dorothy's Retirement Party, 1969.

OF MARY BLAIR DESTINY

Dorothy H. Bryan, 1909 - 1997

Dorothy Bryan and granddaughter Mary Blair Peterson (Mirabal), 1974

Dorothy Bryan and her "Magnificent Seven" at granddaughter Theresa's 1985 wedding. Front Row: Marbury, Josephine, Mary Blair.
Back Row: Dottie, Dorothy, Elizabeth, Trish, Kathleen.

Zimmer & Company Tobacco Shipping Label, Maclin-Zimmer-McGill Tobacco Company, Petersburg, Virginia.

OF MARY BLAIR DESTINY

Dorothy Bryan in 1986, enjoying her seat in the parlor of 244 S. Sycamore Street, Petersburg, Virginia, the former Zimmer family home. At age 76, this was the first and only time she would enter, as the stately home housed church offices at that time and was open to the public.

ERIN L. RICHMAN

"Your expressions of appreciation were more than I deserve. I accept them with gratitude, and feel that this is a new beginning (I might make it to a hundred), with the past a closed book except for the good times."

Love,
Mother/Granny
80th Birthday, 1989

CPSIA information can be obtained
at www.ICGtesting.com
Printed in the USA
BVHW060235070519
547503BV00004B/5/P